WESTERN

THE COWBOY'S HOMECOMING

—

DONNA ALWARD

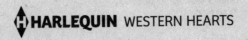

Recycling programs
for this product may
not exist in your area.

⊕HARLEQUIN® WESTERN HEARTS

ISBN-13: 978-1-335-50773-0

The Cowboy's Homecoming
First published in 2015.
This edition published in 2020.
Copyright © 2015 by Donna Alward

This edition published by arrangement with Harlequin Books S.A.

For questions and comments about the quality of this book,
please contact us at CustomerService@Harlequin.com.

Harlequin Enterprises ULC
22 Adelaide St. West, 40th Floor
Toronto, Ontario M5H 4E3, Canada
www.Harlequin.com

Printed in U.S.A.

Donna Alward lives on Canada's east coast with her family, which includes her husband, a couple of kids, a senior dog and two crazy cats. Her heartwarming stories of love, hope and homecoming have been translated into several languages, hit bestseller lists and won awards, but her favorite thing is hearing from readers! When she's not writing she enjoys reading (of course), knitting, gardening, cooking... and she is a *Masterpiece Theatre* addict. You can visit her on the web at donnaalward.com and join her mailing list at donnaalward.com/newsletter.

Chapter 1

Crooked Valley Ranch had changed since Rylan had last been here.

He drove slowly up the driveway, the Ford 4x4 and hybrid camper he towed behind moving easily over the gravel lane, not a pothole to be seen. Duke must have had it leveled this spring, he mused.

Ry touched the brakes and stared at the house. A fresh coat of white paint was on the front porch and flowers bloomed in a profusion of color in front of crisscross lattice skirting. The barns could use a new coat of paint as well, but there was an air of neatness and organization that had been missing before, too. It looked as if his sister hadn't been kidding. Crooked Valley Ranch was on its way up.

"I'll be damned," he breathed, a smile touching his lips. He never would have thought his dyed-in-the-wool military brother, Duke, would turn out to be a rancher. But if outward appearances meant anything, Duke was doing a damned good job revitalizing their granddad's spread.

Rylan scowled a little, chafing against the demand-presented-as-a-request he'd received from Lacey. Duke was staying on at Crooked Valley. Hell, he was married and had a baby on the way—a family to support. Lacey had taken over the administration aspect of the operation, and she and the ranch manager, Quinn Solomon, were planning a June wedding. Joe Duggan's will required all three of his grandchildren to take their place at the ranch before the year was up or else the place would be sold. Lacey had totally guilted him into coming "home," as she'd put it.

"It's not forever," she'd assured him. "Just use this as your home base. That's all we ask. We've never asked anything else of you, Rylan. Please help us keep it in the family.

Once everything's settled, Duke and I will find a way to buy out your third."

Roots. He tried to avoid them whenever he could. Still, it kind of stung that Lacey had just dismissed him as having no interest in the ranch. Not that he wanted his part of it, but that they hadn't expected it of him. No one ever expected anything of him, did they? He should have been used to it by now.

He pulled into a big vacant spot next to the horse barn and cut the engine, which also cut out the comforting sounds of the music he'd had blaring on the radio during the drive from Wyoming.

Truth was, he'd known since February that this day was coming.

His arrival must have made some noise, because a little girl came rushing out of the barn, brown curls bobbing. Amber, Quinn's daughter. Rylan grinned. Little-known secret: he liked kids. Kids were easy, and honest, and thought being a grown-up meant doing what you wanted to do and not what someone told you. At least with kids, he never had his choices judged. To them, he was "cool."

"Hey, short stuff!" He hopped out of the cab and slammed the door.

"Hi," she offered, but stopped short, tilted her head and stared at him. "Are you going to be my Uncle Ry now?"

Yep, blunt honesty. He grinned back at her. "Looks that way. I'm okay with it if you are."

She nodded. "I gots a dog. Her name is Molly."

"Congratulations."

With a happy giggle, Amber turned around to run back to the barn, but stopped when she saw Quinn coming around the corner. Rylan liked Quinn, and he was happy for his sister. They'd make this work out somehow... He knew his brother and sister didn't realize it, but he actually did care about their happiness. That was the only reason he'd come back.

That and the heavy sense of inevitability that told him he probably should face his demons at some point.

And then a blond head appeared, the streaky strands of hair twisted back in a braid. His gut clenched. Maybe it wasn't her. Maybe he could be that lucky. He wasn't ready for the confrontation he knew would be coming.

The woman came around beside Quinn,

both of them talking, and he recognized the long legs, curvy figure and slight sway to her walk. Kailey Brandt. He held back a groan. Why did she have to be here right at this particular moment? Why couldn't he have had time to prepare, to work out something to say?

He hadn't spoken to her since Valentine's Day, when she'd hopped into his truck and had gone back to the motel with him after the benefit dance at the Silver Dollar. He'd slipped out the morning after, before she woke. It had been a coward's move and one he wasn't proud of. He figured he deserved whatever she would sling his way. He'd just hoped to avoid it for a little while longer.

"Daddy, Uncle Ry's here!" Amber's sweet voice broke the silence and both Quinn and Kailey looked up. Quinn's face broke out into a smile while Kailey's…

Damn. His gut twisted again. She looked ready to commit murder.

"Rylan," Quinn greeted him, holding out a hand. "Glad you're finally here."

Rylan shook his hand. "Me, too, Quinn. Congratulations on your engagement. Glad my sister isn't marrying some pansy-ass."

Quinn laughed. "To the point. And a compliment, I think."

"It is."

His gaze slid over to Kailey. Her lips were set in a thin, unrelenting line, her eyes as cold as January ice.

"Hello, Kailey."

She looked down at Amber, who was within earshot, then pasted on the falsest smile he'd ever seen. "Why, hello, stranger."

Quinn frowned, looking from Rylan to Kailey and back to Rylan again. "Okay, I'm just a guy and even I can tell there's some friction here. What's going on?"

Kailey patted Quinn's arm. "Nothing. Nothing at all. I'd better get back home now. Chores to do and stuff."

Without so much as a nod goodbye, Kailey marched off in the direction of her truck. Rylan noticed it was a year or two newer than his, a V8 with a crew cab and lots of power to tow a trailer full of stock. He had no doubt she could do it, too. She was the prettiest girl he'd ever seen. And one of the toughest and most capable.

Quinn's voice was low. "That have something to do with Valentine's Day?"

No sense making excuses. Rylan met his gaze evenly. "Probably," he admitted.

Amber bounced away to play with Lacey's pup, Ranger, and Quinn blew out a breath. "You know, Lacey insisted that you guys were adults. That I needed to let things be. But let me tell you this. That girl is one of my best friends."

"Warning received," Rylan acknowledged. "I'll make things right. I don't have any intention of hurting her, Quinn."

"Intentions are funny things," Quinn replied. But he let the matter drop, thankfully. "Have you been inside to see your sister yet?"

"No."

"She's thrilled you're here. Just so you know."

Unease settled over Rylan again. He'd come to Crooked Valley as requested, but he fully intended to do his own thing and on his own schedule. That was the agreement. None of this convincing-him-to-stay crap. He'd be on the road most of the summer anyway, hitting as many rodeos as possible in his run for the National Finals title. He had a real chance this year and he wasn't about to blow it.

"I'll park the trailer and make my way up in a bit."

Quinn nodded. "I'll see you later then."

He gave Ry a clap on the shoulder before moving on toward the rambling farmhouse. Rylan looked after him, vague memories stirring in his brain. He'd been little but he still remembered. He remembered Grampa Joe and Grandma Eileen and learning to ride the horses and the sound of his dad's laughter. Grandma had made the best chocolate cake he'd ever had, and Grampa Joe had bought Ry a pony to ride since he was younger and smaller than Duke. The pony's name had been Daisy and he'd doted on her from the first moment, feeding her treats of apples and carrots, and brushing her every day.

His early childhood had been absolutely perfect.

There were other memories, too. He remembered how it had felt to hear the news that his father was never coming home. It had been incomprehensible to imagine a world where Dad wouldn't come thumping in, dropping his duffel and looking so tall and important in his uniform. Ry had spent hours in the barns, sitting with the horses, smelling their warm, pungent hides and trying to make sense of it all. He'd told Daisy all his feelings, burying his face in her coarse mane when things got to be too much for him to understand.

And then even that had been taken away when their mother had moved them to Helena and that small house on a postage-stamp lot. The city, for God's sake. No fields, no chocolate cake and no Daisy.

He would never invest that much of himself in a place again. No commitments meant no disappointments, and that was just how he liked it.

He got back in the truck and found a nice level spot to park his camper.

Kailey had thought a lot about what she'd say to Rylan Duggan the next time she saw him. She'd also known that Lacey and Duke had asked him to come to Crooked Valley. His presence here would ensure that the ranch stayed in the family, and with two of the three Duggan siblings invested in it now, his agreement was especially important. She understood that.

But to her knowledge he hadn't agreed, and he certainly hadn't advised anyone of his arrival. He'd just shown up, wearing those faded jeans and a cocky grin that had made her traitorous body stand up straight and pay attention.

She hated him for that. Almost as much as she hated that she was just that weak to fall for a sexy smile and fine ass. Well, falling for it and acting on it were two different things. He wouldn't get the chance to burn her again.

Dust puffed up in clouds behind her tires as she drove along a dirt road parallel to the Brandt ranch. Just beyond the next ridge was the bend in the Crooked Valley Creek, where the water slowed, creating the perfect summer swimming hole. She needed some peace and quiet, some tranquility, before she went home. The last thing she wanted to do was take this mood inside.

Sometimes it really sucked being in her late twenties and still living with her parents. Yet it made no sense to do otherwise, when she spent 90 percent of her time working the ranch. The ranch that was going to be hers someday. That had always been perfectly clear. She was an only child. Without her, the ranch would have to be sold.

She loved Brandt Ranch. She truly did.

But having the weight of it on her shoulders had come with a price.

Finally, she slowed and pulled off the dirt road, driving carefully down a path that was no more than two tire tracks through the grass. It opened up into a wide, grassy knoll that led to the water. As she climbed out of the truck, she could hear the comforting warble of the creek and the sound of the birds in the nearby trees and bushes.

She picked her way down the bank to the edge of the water and dipped her fingers in. "Brrr." She shivered and pulled her hand back out. It was only May and the creek was higher than usual, fed by the runoff from the mountains. There'd be no swimming today.

But the sun was warm and there wasn't a soul around for miles. She closed her eyes and rolled her shoulders, trying to ease the tension out of the tight muscles, but she could only see Rylan in her mind, his weight resting on one hip, looking calm and sexy and as if he didn't have a care in the world.

It was her own stupid fault. She'd antici-pated a no-strings night of fun when they'd hooked up a few months ago. She'd needed it after putting on an "I'm so over it" show for Colt Black. No one had known how serious their relationship had been, or how hurt she'd been when he'd rebounded so quickly and found another girl. Newly single and at the benefit for Quinn and Amber, Colt had danced with her and asked if they could be friends again.

And to demonstrate how very over him she was, she'd flirted with Rylan, danced with him, fallen under his spell despite herself. By the time she'd awakened in an empty bed the next morning, she'd fallen for him. Hard. And she'd seen Rylan Duggan for who he really was.

A heartless bastard.

Worse than that, she hated herself for her moment of weakness. Maybe Rylan had left her high and dry, but she'd put herself in that position all on her own. She'd rather just forget that whole night had ever happened.

Letting out a huge sigh, Kailey sank into the warm grass and lay back against the ground, letting it cushion her body as she turned her face up to the sun. The water was cold, but the sun's rays were gloriously hot. She unbuttoned her plaid shirt, letting the fabric fall away from her chest and abdomen, exposing her skin to the sun. She let the rays soak in, restoring her calm and her confidence. It made her feel feminine, when so often she felt like one of the guys, smelling like the barn and sweat. She loved every second of it, but once in a while a woman liked to feel like a woman.

She'd definitely felt like a woman in Rylan Duggan's arms. After he'd left her at the motel, she'd come to the conclusion that she not only didn't need Rylan, but she didn't need anyone at all. Maybe someday the right man would come along and sweep her off her feet, treat her the way she should be treated. Like an equal. With respect. Someone who wouldn't mind that she already was tied down—to her ranch.

Kailey sighed heavily, a deep, cleansing breath. And if her Prince Charming never showed up, well, that was all right, too. She was fine just the way she was.

Except she sometimes wondered if that were true. First it had been Carrie, now Lacey. Both deliriously happy. And somehow Kailey felt as if she was missing out on something important.

One thing she knew for sure, she thought, as she stretched out in the sun. Rylan Duggan was *not* the thing she was missing out on. She'd learned her lesson there.

If she had her way, he'd be hitting the road for his next rodeo before any of them had time to catch their breath. In and out of her life as quickly as he had been the last time.

On Rylan's first night home, Lacey pulled out all the stops, just as Ry had known she would. Duke and Carrie came for dinner, and Quinn and Amber practically lived at the ranch, though the official move-in wasn't until after the wedding in June. Lacey had made potato salad and Caesar salad, and Quinn was grilling rib-eyes for the prodigal celebration. It was nice but unnecessary. He didn't want any fuss made.

Good luck with that.

They had asked all sorts of questions about Rylan's latest rodeo conquests and were well into the meal when Duke brought up the subject of Rylan's camper.

"I noticed you set up your RV," Duke said as he cut into his steak. "That's a great little rig. You must like it when you're traveling."

Rylan nodded. "It's smaller than some, but there's only one of me. Doesn't take long to set up and suits me just fine." Truthfully, he'd had something bigger but it had been a pain in the ass, heavier to haul, more space than he'd needed. He'd sold it in February and had bought the smaller set-up. On the heels of his latest win, he'd been flush with cash for a few weeks.

Including over Valentine's Day.

"I made up the spare room with fresh sheets," Lacey broke in, handing a basket of buns to Quinn. "Same one you slept in at Christmas."

Rylan put down his fork. "Not necessary, sis." He smiled. "I'm happy in the camper."

"Rylan Joseph Duggan. You are not sleeping in a camper!"

He raised one eyebrow as all eyes turned to look at her. "Wow," Quinn said. "You've got the mother voice down cold."

"Can I sleep in your camper, Uncle Ry?" Amber speared a piece of steak that her father had cut for her. "I's never been camping."

"We'll see, pumpkin."

Lacey regarded him with disapproval. "Rylan, really. There's no need to sleep in the yard when there's a perfectly good room here with your name on it."

Right. Just what he needed. To horn in on her relationship with Quinn. Maybe the manager hadn't formally moved in yet, but it was clear as the nose on Rylan's face that the three of them had a cozy little vibe going on. Besides, the wedding was in less than a month. The last thing he wanted was to be smack in the middle of their newlywed love nest.

"I like it," he contradicted mildly. "I've got my own space. My own privacy. And I won't be invading your privacy either."

"There's a much better mattress on the bed upstairs." Lacey frowned. "You surely didn't come all this way to sleep in that contraption."

"I prefer it."

"What if you have to go to the bathroom in the night?"

Rylan couldn't help it. He burst out laughing and smiles bloomed on faces around the table. "Really? What am I, five?"

Amber lifted her chin. "You can't be five, Uncle Ry. I'm gonna be five in two weeks." She rolled her eyes.

"See?" He reached over and ruffled Amber's hair. "Five, huh? Guess that means you start school in September."

"Real school," she replied importantly.

Amber's insertion into the conversation

had mollified Lacey a little bit. "You're sure?" she asked. "There's lots of room."

"I'm sure. I also know how to do my own laundry. Make food."

Quinn stepped in. "You're going to want to take advantage of the food thing. Your sister's a heck of a cook." Rylan watched as Quinn turned a tender gaze on his fiancée. "Even when you don't want it, she's going to press food on you. You might as well accept it and enjoy."

Lacey turned pleading eyes on him. "Yes, Rylan, please eat your meals here."

"I can probably do that," he conceded. The small concession would get her off his back, and he'd eat a lot better than if he cooked for himself.

Duke joined the conversation. "You're always welcome at the bunkhouse, too, Ry. Carrie and I have room. At least until the baby comes."

Which would be in a few months. Carrie was already glowing with motherhood, her hand resting on her rounded belly. And Rylan smiled through it all, feeling incredibly claustrophobic and smothered.

"I'll stick to the camper for now, but thanks for the invites." His jaw felt tight and he forced himself to relax it. "Heck, I'm going to be rodeoing a fair bit of the time anyway. Easier to just hook up and go, you know?"

This would be his home base. No commitments, no ties. He was still going to run this life the way he had for the past several years. On his terms, coming and going as he pleased.

He knew at times it must have seemed as if he didn't care for his family, but nothing could have been further from the truth. That he was here was proof of that. He wanted this for them, if it was what would make them happy, and he was strangely happy that he could finally do something right rather than merely being an afterthought.

He just hoped they could accept that he needed to run his life his own way, too, and understand when the time came for him to leave again.

Chapter 2

Kailey stared in the boutique's mirror and had to admit that Lacey had fantastic taste.

The bridesmaid dress was turquoise blue, a slightly brighter shade than a robin's egg. The light material draped and flowed in an utterly feminine way, fluttering to a hem just above her knees. It was strapless, leaving Kailey's shoulders bare, and she realized she was going to have to rectify the farmer tan she had from working outside in T-shirts by employing some self-tanner. But she loved it. She completely and utterly loved it.

Lacey came back to the dressing room with a box in her hands. "Oh my gosh!

That's so beautiful on you!" She put the box on a padded seat and put her hands to her mouth. "Oh, Kailey. You're stunning."

Kailey felt a blush climb her cheeks. Not that she didn't like dressing up for a night out, because she did. Occasionally it was nice to feel like a girl. But this was different. It felt so formal. So…foreign. The only wedding she'd been in before had been Duke and Carrie's, and that had been so low-key that she'd just worn a pretty red dress from her closet and a flower in her hair.

"It's not too much?" Kailey looked down, hitched up the bodice just a touch. She had to admit, she liked the way the fabric crisscrossed her breasts and waist.

"It's perfect." Lacey beamed at her. "And don't worry about wearing heels you'll break your neck in. Here. I got you these. My present to you."

Lacey picked up the box again and handed it to Kailey.

Kailey opened the lid and found a gorgeous pair of cowboy boots nestled inside, with matching blue accents inlaid on the boot shaft.

"Wow. Just…wow."

"I figured you might not wear the dress

again, but you might find some use for these."

Kailey took the first one out of the box and slid it on. It was a perfect fit. "There is nothing more comfortable than a good pair of boots," she decreed, looking up at Lacey and smiling.

"I'm going to be wearing a pair, too," Lacey replied. "Under my dress."

Kailey had seen Lacey's dress. It was sweet, in a similar style to Kailey's only long and white and with frothy light material on the overskirt. Simple and very, very sweet—just like the bride. "The boots can be your something blue," Kailey suggested, and Lacey grinned.

"I might have thought of that." She looked at Kailey. "So what do you think? Alterations? Or is it fine as is?"

It fit perfectly. "I think we can take this home today, don't you?"

Lacey nodded. "I can't believe it's only a few weeks away. Sometimes it feels like it's all happened so fast, and other times it seems to be taking so long!"

Kailey smiled in return, though it felt forced. She kind of understood what Lacey meant but in the totally opposite way. Valentine's Day seemed like ages ago, yet the time from then to now had gone so fast. Quinn and Lacey had been busy falling in love and she'd…

She'd been busy, all right. Thinking she'd seen something in Rylan Duggan that didn't exist. Thinking he was…different.

"I should change," she suggested, annoyed that she'd allowed Rylan to sneak into her thoughts. "We still have errands to run, right?"

With two and a half weeks until the big day, Kailey was spending more time than usual away from the ranch, fulfilling her maid of honor duties. Not that she minded, but it was a busy time of year. They'd be making the first cut of hay soon, not to mention rodeo season picking up. She didn't often travel with the stock, but she had the final say on which animals traveled and she was in charge of making the arrangements.

"Right," Lacey replied, taking the boots from Kailey as she reluctantly removed them. "K, you're going to knock Rylan's socks off in that dress."

Kailey scowled. "That is so not the objective."

"Oh, of course not." Lacey's face looked

a little too innocent to be believed. "But you have to admit it's a nice little side benefit."

"Whose side are you on, anyway?" Kailey turned her back so Lacey could undo the hook and eye at the top of the zipper.

"Hey, I love my brother. Don't get me wrong." Lacey's fingers were cool against Kailey's skin as she undid the clasp. "But that doesn't mean I agree with everything he does. Like hurt my new best friend."

Kailey swallowed thickly. She loved it in Gibson, had lived here all her life. And she and Carrie had been good friends for years. But she had to admit, that with the exception of Rylan, she was very, very glad that the Duggan siblings had come to live at Crooked Valley. Duke and Lacey's friendship had become really important to her.

"That's sweet," she said, trying to make her voice sound breezy. "But you don't have to worry about me. That's water under the bridge."

"I'm glad to hear it."

Ouch. Not that she mistook Lacey's meaning. Clearly the family was aware of what had happened on Valentine's Day. And she knew that all Lacey meant was that she was glad Kailey had moved on. But it stung a little, too, that Lacey was glad there was nothing between them. It felt as if the Duggans wouldn't support her having a relationship with Rylan… After all, blood was thicker than water. Maybe they thought she wasn't good enough for their little brother.

She locked herself in the changing room and frowned. What the heck was wrong with her, thinking like that? She didn't *want* a relationship with Rylan, for Pete's sake! What she wanted was for him to satisfy his inheritance requirement and then just leave again.

And good enough? She pulled on her jeans and zipped them, her movements quick and efficient. Jeez, she let one guy catalogue all her faults as a girlfriend and suddenly she doubted herself. Honestly, there were days she wished she'd never met Colt Black and his charming face. Or Rylan and his charming face, too. Boy, she was a sucker for the lookers, wasn't she?

But today that didn't matter. Today was about Lacey's wedding, so after she put the dress in the garment bag and paid the balance at the counter, she and Lacey started back to Gibson for lunch. This afternoon they had appointments to put in the final order for the cake and flowers. Lacey was the perfect blushing bride-to-be, radiant and happy during the preparations. There hadn't been a single bridezilla moment, and for that Kailey was eternally grateful.

The Horseshoe Diner was doing a bustling business over the lunch hour, and Kailey and Lacey found themselves at a table near the back, close to where the ancient jukebox sat. Lacey, being ever conscious of fitting into her wedding dress, ordered a salad with dressing on the side. Kailey didn't worry so much about what she ate, considering the physical labor she did each day. She ordered a cheeseburger with bacon and hot peppers and then, at Lacey's horrified expression, asked for a side salad instead of fries.

She would not look at her watch and worry about chores. She deserved a day off. This was Lacey's wedding after all. Things could run without her for a few hours.

Their food came as they were discussing the merits of having both a white and chocolate layer in the wedding cake. Kailey was just considering the best way to pick up her cheeseburger when the front door swung open and Rylan and Quinn strode through.

Lacey had her back to the door, so it was

Kailey who saw them first, and her heart sank as she watched Quinn scan the room for an empty table. There weren't any that Kailey could see, and she looked down, hoping the pair wouldn't see them sitting there. Not that she'd mind Quinn, but Rylan? No thanks.

No such luck. A quick glance showed her that they were on their way over, Quinn leading the way with a big smile. Of course he was smiling. Lacey was there. Rylan didn't look quite as pleased. Apparently he wasn't looking forward to seeing her any more than she was looking forward to seeing him.

"Is there room for two more here?" Quinn asked, and Lacey's head snapped up in surprise, her face flushing with pleasure.

"Of course there is!" She patted the chair next to her. "Our food just arrived. I'm sure yours won't take long."

Quinn gave her a quick kiss and sat while Rylan stood by Lacey's chair. "May I?" he asked quietly, politely. Unenthusiastically.

"Be my guest," she answered coolly, wishing now that she'd gotten the fries. And a big soda. And a hot fudge sundae to bury her head in.

"Thanks," he murmured and took the seat beside her.

He and Quinn ordered and Kailey noticed that Lacey wasn't eating, instead saving her salad for when everyone had their food. She looked longingly at her burger, still hot from the grill, the scent of the beef so delectable her stomach growled in anticipation. With a little chuckle, Rylan leaned over. "Eat it. It won't be as good cold."

"That would be rude," she replied, trying to ignore the delicious shiver that skittered down her spine at the quiet words uttered so closely to her ear.

"Not if we say it's not." He sat back, picked up his glass of water and took a sip. "Seriously. Eat. Don't let us interrupt your lunch."

She still felt awkward, but she picked up the burger—she needed both hands—and took a first delicious bite. Closed her eyes and simply enjoyed the explosion of flavor happening inside her mouth.

When she opened her eyes again, Rylan was watching her, a look of fascination on his face, and something more, too. Hunger. For her? Or for her lunch? She grabbed her paper napkin and scrubbed it across her lips, looking away from him.

"It's that good, is it?" he asked, the note of teasing slightly strained.

"Always," she replied, taking a drink of water. "I'm afraid I'm not one of those fancy dish people with the fresh this and that, and herb and goat stuff and whatever. A good beef burger with bacon and cheese and some jalapenos and I'm a happy girl."

"Not champagne tastes then."

She met his eyes evenly. "Not really. My tastes tend to be rather…ordinary."

She could see in his eyes when he got her meaning, and she felt a little bit small for implanting the barb in such an innocuous way.

She hid by taking another bite of her burger while Quinn and Lacey chatted about wedding stuff.

Moments later Quinn's and Rylan's meals arrived, and she watched with envy as Rylan picked up a crispy fry and dipped it in a little dish of ketchup. He'd ordered a club sandwich, and didn't waste any time helping himself. Likewise, Quinn picked up his pulled-pork bun and took a hearty bite. Out of sorts, Kailey wondered why men could order such meals and it was all manly and if a woman did the same thing, she got sideways looks. It was a stupid double standard. Especially considering what her daily calorie burn tended to be. Scowling, she took another huge bite of her burger.

"You should see Kailey's dress." Lacey's sweet voice interrupted the meal, and Kailey nearly dropped the half of the burger she had left in her hands while she chewed what had ended up being too big a bite. "She looks beautiful. The color is just perfect."

Kailey struggled to finish chewing and finally swallowed the mouthful, feeling as if she had no table manners at all. "Lace, I'm not sure the guys are interested in bridesmaid dresses, you know?"

Quinn put his arm along the back of Lacey's chair. "Aw, there's nothing wrong with being excited about the wedding," he replied, looking at Lacey with such devotion it was nearly sickening.

Kailey wasn't usually so cynical. Maybe it was because Rylan was beside her. And Rylan had been the one to leave her alone in a motel room after what was the most romantic night of the year—Valentine's Day. Perhaps if it had been underwhelming, it wouldn't be so difficult to put in the past.

Trouble was it had been amazing. Rock-her-world amazing.

Kailey had often wondered if she should trust her own judgment with men, and the incident with Rylan pretty much had cemented the answer.

She was better off sticking to horses and bulls.

"What color is it?"

Rylan asked the question and she really, really wished he hadn't. "Blue," she answered. "It's blue."

Lacey laughed. "You can't just say blue. There are lots of blues out there." She turned her attention to Rylan. "It's kind of a turquoisey sky blue. It looks great with her hair and tan."

Kailey put her forehead on her hand. Her tan? Really? Because she was only tanned around her neck and from the biceps down… like every other rancher in these parts.

"Sounds nice," Rylan answered.

Lacey and Quinn started talking about something to do with Amber, leaving Rylan and Kailey silent on their side of the table again.

"Sorry," he offered quietly, eating another fry. "If I'd known you guys were here, I would have suggested somewhere else."

"It's just awkward, that's all. We're going to run into each other occasionally. We might as well get used to it."

She wiped her fingers on her napkin, then picked up her fork and speared a slice of cucumber from her salad.

"Kailey...I'm sorry."

"For?" She crunched the cucumber, determined to ignore the weird flutterings in her tummy.

"For being such a jerk that morning."

She looked up quickly, checked to see if Quinn or Lacey had heard. Luckily, they were still engrossed in their own conversation. "This isn't the place to discuss it."

"I get the feeling you don't want to discuss it at all, and that's fine. But I do owe you the apology."

Dammit. It was easier to hate him when he wasn't doing the right thing.

Scratch that. The right thing would have been sticking around, at least until coffee. They could have agreed to go their separate ways or...whatever.

"Noted." She stuck her fork savagely into the lettuce.

"Noted, but not accepted?" he asked. "I mean it, Kailey. I was totally in the wrong. Wouldn't it be better if we could get along? As you said, we're going to run into each other. And possibly more than occasionally. I'd like to put it behind us."

She would, too, but she wasn't sure she could until she understood why. Why had he felt the need to rush out before sunrise? Or was he really just a love 'em and leave 'em kind of guy? She'd certainly seen that type before…though she hadn't pegged Rylan as that kind. On top of Colt's rather quick moving on, it had left her feeling, well, *disposable*. Not worth the trouble of sticking around, even for breakfast.

Sitting in the diner with a lunchtime crowd audience didn't seem the right time or place to ask him why. But he was right. Their ranches were side by side. She was good friends with Carrie and Quinn, and Rylan's brother and sister.

Then there was the fact that he wasn't planning on staying at Crooked Valley forever. He was here to fulfill the terms of his grandfather's will, so Lacey and Duke could keep the ranch in the family. Surely she could suck up her personal feelings for a few months. Couldn't she? She'd gotten pretty good at hiding her feelings over the years. She'd had to when she'd taken a bigger role at the ranch and had become the boss of a largely male workforce.

"Consider it behind us," she replied, pushing away her salad. She really wished Lacey would get a move on. Not that she was in the mood for more wedding details, but it would get her away from Rylan.

Rylan, whose gaze she could feel glued to the side of her face. When she couldn't stand it anymore, she sighed.

"What?"

"Thank you," he said simply.

She looked at him and felt her animosity threaten to abandon her. He didn't look cocky or insincere in any way. In fact, his eyes were completely earnest and his lips open just a little, so she could get the full effect of their bowed shape. The bottom one was just a little fuller than the top, and she remembered them being surprisingly soft and...capable.

He was as attractive as ever, but she'd learned her lesson and learned it well. Rylan Duggan was trouble, and trouble was the last thing she needed.

"You're welcome."

Lacey was finally finishing up her salad and Kailey figured she might escape without having to speak to him again, but once more Rylan picked up a new thread of conversation.

"I could use some advice," he said, pushing away his plate. All that was left on it were the four toothpicks that had held his sandwich together, and the little dish that had contained his ketchup.

"Advice about what?" she asked. She hoped to God it wasn't anything personal. An apology was one thing. But they hadn't made that many amends yet.

"On the stock situation at Crooked Valley."

That made her sit back. "Oh?"

He kept his voice low. "Quinn and I have been talking. He's doing okay, but really, Quinn's a cattle man. The little stock we've sent to competition has been handled by Randy. And I know Brandt stock. It's topnotch. I wanted to run some ideas past you."

Nothing he might have said would have surprised her more. On one hand, it was nice to know he respected her knowledge and opinion.

On the other hand, it made her wonder if the apology had really been meant to soften her up into giving him free advice.

Well, either way, it wouldn't hurt to state the obvious. "What Crooked Valley needs is some new breeding stock. A new stud, a couple of mares. But mostly a good stud that you can make some money off of breeding fees. That'll help pad your program so you can grow it."

"That's what I thought." He frowned.

"And Quinn probably knows that, too, but truth of the matter is Crooked Valley can't afford to outlay that much money right now. It's risky, even if the money was in the account. Am I right?"

He nodded. "Yes. According to Duke, our grandfather thought it would be fun to breed some rodeo stock. But it was more of a side thing than a focus, and it's never paid its way or lived up to its potential."

"I know Quinn and Duke have talked about selling it off." Kailey made herself smile. What she'd said about potential was absolutely correct. There were a few mares in the stables that she'd love to get her hands on, breed them with Big Boy. If the Duggans did decide to call this side of the operation quits, she hoped she could get first dibs on some of the unrealized potential in the barn before it went to auction.

"I don't think we're at that point yet."

Did he realize he'd said *we*? He was a temporary addition to the Crooked Valley operation, wasn't he? Or perhaps he used the concept as cavalierly as he used his women.

And maybe she hadn't quite accepted his apology. She bit down on her lip. It wasn't like her to be this nasty, even in her thoughts. She didn't like it. She didn't like anything that Rylan Duggan made her feel.

Quinn coughed, interrupting their conversation. "Sorry to break this up," he said. "But, Ry, I've got to get back."

"No problem," Kailey replied. "It wasn't anything important."

Rylan got up and reached back in his hip pocket for his wallet. She watched as the muscles in his shoulders and back shifted beneath his shirt, remembering what those very muscles looked like without the covering of cotton. He took out some bills and threw them on the table. "Lunch is on me, ladies. Enjoy the rest of your afternoon."

Kailey's face flamed. He was smiling his charming smile and smoothing everything over, wasn't he? And it would be so easy to fall for that again.

Instead, she reached inside her purse, took out a twenty and dropped it on the table before picking up one of his bills and handing it back to him.

"I can pay my own way," she said quietly, and without looking back, headed for the exit.

Kailey strode to Lacey's car, anxious to get going and away from Rylan but trying to look more purposeful than actually running away. That was what he did, not her.

Her breath hitched a little, surprising her, and she gulped, trying to shut down the flood of emotion. She wasn't acting like herself. The Kailey she knew was able to let things roll off her like water off a duck's back. She took things in stride, put them in perspective.

That she couldn't in this one particular instance bugged the hell out of her.

"Hey, wait up!" Lacey's quick steps sounded behind her and Kailey, almost to the car, slowed.

Lacey was slightly out of breath. "Did someone light your tail on fire or what?

And what was that whole deal with the bill, anyway?"

"I'm sorry." Kailey looked at Lacey and wanted to confide, yet held back. This was Rylan's sister. Blood did run thicker than water, or so she'd heard. "I shouldn't let it get to me so much."

"You really don't like Ry, do you?" Lacey put her handbag over her shoulder and studied Kailey.

It was probably the opposite—that she'd liked him too much. "It's not that…" Her voice trailed off, unsure of how to explain.

Over Lacey's shoulder, she saw Quinn and Rylan hop into Quinn's truck and pull away from the curb.

She sighed. "How much do you know about Valentine's Day?" Kailey asked her friend.

Lacey grinned. "I know that as I was leaving with Quinn, you were leaving with Rylan."

That's right. There'd been another, more successful, romance budding back in February. One that had ended with a far better result. "You went home with Quinn, and I had a romantic night at the Shady Pines Motel. With your brother."

Lacey blushed a little. "I know, I know," she said, flapping her hand as Kailey lifted an eyebrow. "I asked."

"I won't go into the gory details." Kailey would spare Lacey that trauma. No one wanted to think of their brother that way! "But here's the thing. I met Rylan at Christmas when he spent the holiday with your family. He's a good-looking guy, Lace. Charming, too. I'd be lying if I said I hadn't been interested. I'd been seeing someone off and on, but that had gone south in a big way. So when he was back less than two months later, and we were both at that Valentine's Day dance…"

"One thing led to another."

"It certainly did. It wasn't something I'm in the habit of doing, either. I was more interested than I probably let on." She gulped. It had sort of been…revenge sex. It just hadn't been with someone random. She'd chosen. She'd chosen Ry.

"He didn't return the sentiment?"

Kailey looked her friend straight in the eye. "Maybe we can finish this conversation in the car? Away from public consumption?"

At Lacey's nod, they got inside the little sedan. Kailey turned in the passenger seat and faced her friend. She had to be honest here, even if Rylan was Lacey's baby brother.

"Okay," she continued. "When I woke up, he'd taken his things and checked out. His truck was gone…it was like he had never been there."

Now Lacey frowned, a wrinkle forming between her perfectly groomed eyebrows. "He ran?"

"Like he couldn't get away fast enough. And he hadn't left enough cash with the room key, so I had to pay the difference."

It had been the singularly most humiliating moment of her life. If he'd hung around, she might have been able to avoid going to the office and seeing Lyle Tucker behind the desk. The small smirk on his face had only added insult to injury as far as Kailey was concerned. It was enough to turn her off romance for a good long while.

"Oh, ouch," Lacey said, frowning. "Hey, I love Ry. He's my brother. But that was pretty crappy behavior."

"Yeah, it was." Kailey sighed. "And I know I should get over myself and just…I don't know, put it behind me. Not let it get to me."

Lacey looked far too hopeful for Kailey's liking. "Could it be you still care for him?"

There was a very real chance of that, but Kailey would never admit to it. "I barely know him," she replied. "And I'm very aware of how that makes me sound considering what we shared." And what they hadn't shared. Her shoulders slumped. "I made a mistake, that's all. And I'm trying, really I am. We were chatting about the stock and stuff and doing fine until he insisted on paying the bill." She sent Lacey a sheepish half smile. "I'm afraid it set me off, since he stiffed the motel, you know?"

"Maybe if you just talk to him—"

Kailey cut her off before she could finish the sentence. "No way. What's done is done. It'll be fine. I just need to put on my big-girl panties."

Lacey laughed. "Well, if it makes you feel any better, Duke is Quinn's best man. You won't be paired up for the day or anything."

It didn't. Because that was just for the ceremony, and maybe a few pictures. The rest of the night Duke and Carrie would be pasted together. And Kailey, the maid of honor, would be the old maid of the group.

Ugh.

"Speaking of..." She changed the subject. "Let's get these errands done. We're supposed to be focusing on your wedding, not my romantic drama."

The mention of wedding errands was enough to set the efficient Lacey into action, and they talked about lace versus satin ribbon for the flowers and cake flavors as they headed down Main Street.

It was just too bad Kailey couldn't get Rylan's gray-blue eyes out of her mind, or the sound of his voice. She knew Lacey and Duke needed him to keep the ranch in the family, but honestly she hoped he wasn't around much. Then life could get back to normal.

Chapter 3

Rylan pulled into the Crooked Valley yard at quarter past seven. Too late for dinner—though if he asked, Lacey would probably have leftovers—and still with enough daylight left that he could chill for a bit before falling into bed.

It would be good to move around for a while, loosen up the tight muscles that came from driving the better part of the day. The past two weekends he'd competed, both times in the money, once at the top. But it hadn't been easy, either. He'd twisted his knee a little yesterday during an awkward dismount, and the rides had been tough, beating his body around enough that he felt it through his ribs and shoulders.

But he was home now. And while he wouldn't admit it to Lacey, it was nice to have a home base. Not that working in Wyoming had been bad. His boss had been good to him. Paid him well.

Ry's needs were simple and he'd been careful with his money. As a result he had a rather nice little nest egg built up for a rainy day.

A rainy day that might have arrived. He still had some thinking to do before making any firm decisions. Still, it didn't hurt for a man to have his ear to the ground.

But first he had to get unhitched. He could hear the dogs, Molly and Ranger, barking inside when he hopped out of the truck and moved to disconnect the camper. It took very little time for him to have it level and ready, just the way he liked it.

No one was home, so he went in the back door and emptied his dirty clothes from his duffel into the washing machine. After petting the dogs and putting some water in their bowl, he took a quick scrounge of the fridge and found leftover meatloaf. Ry sliced a huge hunk and put it between two slices of homemade bread for his dinner, then grabbed a beer from the fridge before heading back outside.

It was quiet. Almost too quiet. What he'd really like to do was go for a swim, let the cool water soothe his tired muscles. With more than an hour of daylight left, he shoved the last crust of bread into his mouth, washed it down with the beer, and struck out for the western edge of the property.

He'd discovered the bend in the creek quite by accident a few days after he'd arrived at the ranch. He'd been out riding, familiarizing himself with the place, and he'd started following the creek toward the property line. He knew at some point the land became Brandt property, but he didn't know when and where. It took him a good half hour to make his way to the spot he'd found before, where the rushing, burbling sound faded to a soft lapping. It was wide enough, deep enough to swim. With the warm sun bathing his face, he stepped through the tall grass to the edge and prepared to strip to his briefs.

And halted, with his hands on the button of his jeans. There was already a pile of clothes on the ground, a heap of denim and a pale green T-shirt next to running shoes. Women's running shoes.

He snapped his gaze to the water at just the right moment to see a woman surface in the stillness, parting the water with a soft splash and then swiping her hair back off her face.

Kailey.

His body reacted in a typical way and he shifted his weight to the other foot, unsure of what to do. What were the chances of him getting out of here without attracting her attention? Slim to none, he would imagine. Standing here staring was another ill-advised move… Damn. It didn't really matter what he did, it would be wrong. After leaving Kailey the way he had, he'd come to expect it from her.

He took a step backward and dry grass crackled beneath his feet. Maybe she wouldn't hear. He'd approached after all, and she hadn't been the wiser. But no such luck this time. Her head snapped around and she saw him standing there, next to her mound of clothing, and he could see her blush even though they were several yards apart.

"Sorry," he called. "I'll go."

He'd turned halfway around when her

voice stopped him. "What are you doing here, Rylan?"

He hesitated and faced the pool—and her—again. "I was going to go for a swim. I saw this place a few weeks ago and thought it would be perfect."

"It is. Don't go. I'm done anyway. If you don't mind turning your back for a few minutes, I'll leave you in peace."

He swallowed, hard. Looked down at her clothes. He didn't see any underwear, and he let out a relieved breath. He wasn't sure his body, or his imagination for that matter, could take knowing she was skinny dipping.

"Don't get out on my account. Really, I'll just go back home."

He'd taken two more steps when she called after him. "Are things going to be this awkward between us forever?"

Forever was a long time. He called back, "I'm not staying forever, so I doubt it."

She didn't answer, but he heard a splash and dared to look over his shoulder.

She'd disappeared again. Lord, but the woman knew how to get under his skin. Far more than she realized.

The water parted and she popped up again. *Screw it*, he thought. He was tired and hot and achy, and he wanted a swim. She could stay or she could go, but she didn't own sole rights to the swimming hole.

He went back to where her clothes were and began unbuttoning his shirt. Kailey had switched from treading water to floating on her back. Only little bits of her were exposed. The tips of her breasts in a white bra and he could just see the edge of matching white underwear.

He took off his jeans and was suddenly very self-conscious. Tighty whities left nothing to the imagination. At all.

There was only one thing to do. He jogged to the water and splashed his way in up to his thighs before diving under.

He surfaced with a bellow. "Janey Mac, that's cold!"

He scrubbed the water away from his face and saw Kailey floating nearby, an amused smile on her face. One thing was for sure, the cold water had gone a long way in helping his uncomfortable situation. He shivered as goose bumps popped up on his skin.

"Janey Mac?" she asked, the surface swirling around her as she tread water.

He grinned. "Something I remember my grandfather saying when I was just a little boy. And my gram would always give him this strange look and call him Joseph."

She nodded. "I remember that. I miss them, you know."

He knew it would be strange for him to say "me, too." He hadn't seen his grandparents in years. He'd avoided this place like the plague, had written it off as simply a part of his past. Being here again, though, had brought back a lot of memories. "You knew them better than I did. Of course you miss them."

He gave a little shift of his body and used his arms to propel himself around, not really swimming, but not treading water either. "It's a bit better when you get used to it," he observed, and Kailey nodded.

"I'm kind of dreading getting out. The air is going to be cold."

"Do you come here a lot?" he asked.

"This is my first time swimming this year. It'll be warmer in the middle of summer. Unless we get a really dry season. Then the creek goes down and there's not much good swimming at all."

"I just got back from Washington. Felt like a dip would blow some of the dust off."

She leaned back, let her toes pop out of the water. "You haven't heard of a shower?"

"This sounded nicer."

They were quiet for a few minutes and Ry decided it was one of the strangest silences he'd ever encountered. On one hand, it was surprisingly comfortable. And on the other, he knew she had a zillion burning questions. Probably starting with asking why he'd run out on her that morning. He hoped to God she didn't actually ask.

"How'd you do?" she said finally, as she started to push herself off in a breast stroke.

"Huh?"

"At the rodeo. How'd you do?"

He shrugged, the air cold on his shoulders. "I did all right. In the money."

He'd won, but he wasn't going to brag.

"You're really good. I've seen the standings. And a couple of our guys are pretty excited you've shown up next door. You could probably come over and sign autographs."

Maybe she really was warming up to him after all. Maybe she'd gotten over whatever had been bugging her that day at the diner when she'd refused to let him buy her lunch. "That's pretty generous of you to say," he observed. "Considering."

"Considering what? That I think you're a jerk?"

And just like that she was beneath the water again. The girl could swim like an otter.

She emerged at the other side of the swimming hole. "Maybe it is time for me to go," she said, and struck out for the edge.

"Kailey, I get that you're mad, and you have every right to be. I'm sorry. I have no excuses for my behavior."

Her feet touched bottom and she started walking her way in. "It says something when a guy can't even hang around for breakfast." She was stomping now, making an unholy racket as she splashed her way toward shore. "Or when you stiff the motel on part of your bill."

"Wait, what?" He put his feet on the bottom and stared at her. What was she talking about?

"You underpaid. I had to drop off the room key, which would have been humiliating enough. But there was still twenty bucks owing."

He'd been sure he'd counted out enough twenties before leaving the money on the desk in an envelope he'd found in a drawer in the room.

But it had also been five in the morning. And dark.

She was standing on the edge now, in her white bra and panties. Which theoretically covered as much as any two-piece bathing suit, maybe more. But then there was the issue that it was white. And soaking wet.

And see-through.

"Kailey," he said, his voice rough. "For the love of God, I hope you have a towel."

She stared at him for a few seconds before what he'd said registered. But it was long enough for him to get a good long look at what was beneath the transparent fabric. And long enough for him to remember what it had been like with her back in February in the dim light of the motel room.

Amazing. Incredible. Scary as hell.

It was that last part that kept him grounded, tempered the need pounding through him to have her again. Cold water or not, he knew it was best for both of them if he stayed submerged right now.

She spun away and trotted off to where she'd left her clothes, then bent over to retrieve a towel she'd brought. He groaned a little, wondering if she'd bent over like that on purpose just to torture him.

When she turned around again, she had the towel wrapped around her. Well, around her middle, anyway. It was short and only went to the tops of her thighs. He could still see the lovely, long expanse of leg beneath it.

Kailey Brandt was trouble. And he was starting to believe she didn't realize that about herself.

She was also angry. And beneath that he suspected she might be a little bit hurt. That's what bothered him most of all. He hadn't meant to hurt her. Hadn't known he actually could.

"I'm sorry," he repeated. "Kailey, me leaving that morning was all on me. It had nothing to do with you."

"Really?" Skepticism was ripe in her tone.

"Really," he insisted. What could he say that would be close to the truth but not *the* truth? He was scrambling and the moments strung out until Kailey let out a huff.

"You're a liar, Rylan Duggan. What was it, anyway? Was I too clingy? Too sweet? Did you think I'd expect a proposal in the morning? Was I unsatisfactory as a lover? I mean, I haven't had that complaint before, but sometimes people don't gel for whatever reason and—"

"No!" He cut her off, ran a hand over his wet hair. "Shut up, Kailey. Just shut up."

He started walking out of the water and as he got closer he could see her eyes swimming with tears. "Aw, Kailey…"

She held up her hand. "Just don't. I cry when I'm angry. And right now I'm really wound up."

He reached her and tried not to shiver as the cool evening air touched his wet skin. "You want to know the truth? I liked it. A lot. Too much. And I was afraid that if I didn't get up and leave that morning that I'd end up staying for breakfast. Or longer."

"And would that have been so bad?"

"At the time? Yes."

"Why?"

God, he hated these kinds of conversations. He'd learned long ago that there was no right answer to her kind of question, so he was as honest as he dared to be. "Because I didn't have anything to offer you. I still don't. I'm not the kind of guy who hangs around, Kailey."

"You're here now. At the ranch, I mean."

"But only temporarily. Remember?"

He didn't stick around any one place for long. He liked it much better being free to go where he pleased, when he pleased. He called the shots and made his own choices. It had been a long time since anyone had made them for him. His choices, his consequences. It was easier that way.

He scooted past her and grabbed his shirt from the ground, gave it a shake and pulled it on. His shorts still dripped and there was no way he could put his jeans on over top. If she hadn't been here, he would have simply stripped to the skin and gone for a dip. Now his only option was to stand here and be cold or to take them off and pull on his jeans commando.

"Turn around," he ordered.

"What?"

"Turn around."

He could tell the moment she understood his meaning because her cheeks flushed bright pink. Despite it, she lifted her chin a little. "It's nothing I haven't seen before."

He could mention that he'd pretty much seen everything of hers, too, through that wet underwear, but he didn't. If she was determined to prove a point, he'd oblige. With a shrug he pushed down his shorts and stepped out of them, then reached for his jeans and tugged them on awkwardly. His skin was still wet and the fabric clung to his legs. He finally got them buttoned and carefully zipped.

When he looked up her face was bright red, but she hadn't looked away.

It was better now that he was dressed, and he reached down and grabbed her T-shirt, handing it over. "Here. Get warm."

She dropped her towel and he caught a glimpse of her abdomen, lean and pale compared to the worker's tan on her arms and face. Immediately the green shirt got dark, damp spots on her chest.

What he really wanted to do was spread out his shirt or that towel and lay her down on it. That part hadn't changed. He still found her beautiful, intriguing and sexy as hell. Probably because of her confidence. Or bullheadedness. Two sides of the same coin, he figured.

And then she stripped off her panties and pulled on her jeans and he had to look away. Whatever point she was trying to prove, she'd done it.

"Kailey, I don't want things to be strained. I can't apologize forever. I meant it when I said I was completely at fault. I don't know how else to make amends. What do you want me to do? I'll do it. The last thing I want is to disrupt anything here."

She wadded up her underwear and rolled them into the damp towel. "There's nothing you can do. I don't actually want to keep punishing you for it. I can't seem to help myself."

"I'm not trying to push your buttons."

"I know that. You've gone out of your way to be nice. I just…don't want you to be nice. I don't know what I want, Rylan. I have too much pride for my own good."

He chuckled then. "No wonder we seem to butt heads. All that pride getting in the way."

"What can I say? I have a bit of a chip on my shoulder. I've had to."

He didn't doubt it. He knew for a fact that Kailey was heavily involved in raising Brandt stock, and that took strength and a good amount of backbone. There were still some good old boys who didn't appreciate a woman running ranch operations and didn't like taking orders. It was a load of garbage, in his opinion.

But he guessed that what had happened

on Valentine's Day probably also had gotten around town. He sat down on the grass and patted the spot beside him. "Sit for a minute, instead of looking like you're ready to throttle me."

She hesitated but then sat, pulling her knees close to her chest and wrapping her arms around them. The pose made her look almost childlike, especially with her tawny hair falling over her shoulders in wet ribbons.

"Did what happened with us make things difficult for you?" he asked quietly.

She frowned. "What do you mean?"

"I mean, stiffing the guy for the room was unintentional, but Gibson is small. If what happened got around…" He let the thought hang for a few seconds before continuing. "I know you're a woman operating in a male-dominated world. The last thing you need is rumors about your personal life undermining that."

"I'm not sure if I'm touched by your concern or infuriated that it's even an issue. I'm sure your reputation wouldn't suffer for such a thing. You'd be given *atta boys*. Am I right?"

"It's a stupid double standard, and I hope I didn't play a part in it."

She met his gaze. "Rylan, I'm no angel. I'm in my late twenties and definitely not some delicate, virginal flower. But I certainly don't make a habit of catting around, and I keep my personal life discreet." She sighed. "Or at least I try to."

Rylan hadn't considered this side of things before, and a pang of regret made his heart heavy. When was the last time he'd truly liked someone enough to care what happened the morning after? He honestly couldn't remember. He moved around. Got used to the buckle bunnies who followed the circuit and were looking to put another notch on *their* belts. Up until this year, he'd obliged now and again.

Not since February though. Not since he'd awakened in the dark to find Kailey sleeping beside him. Something had happened. Something that had made him feel wonderful and extremely uncomfortable at the same time.

The urge to stay.

He'd half figured that by leaving the way he did, she'd get a good old-fashioned hate on for him and that would be that. He'd come back to Crooked Valley expecting a cold shoulder. Over and done with, move on.

He could see now his thinking had been flawed. Because Kailey was more hurt and embarrassed than angry, and knowing it brought out every single protective and possessive instinct he had. He wanted to fix it, explain. He wanted… Crap. He wanted to be able to forget about her the way he'd expected her to forget about him. And he couldn't.

That wouldn't do anyone any good, and neither would sitting in the middle of a field in semi-darkness.

"Come on. I'll walk you home," he suggested. "It's getting dark."

"Newsflash, Duggan. You're on Brandt land. I'm already home. Maybe I should walk you back, huh?"

She was so quick, a little feisty, and he liked that about her. A lot. "If you want to kill my reputation with a single blow, sure. Big bad rodeo star needs an escort home in the dark."

Not that he couldn't find a few things to do in the dark with her.

He had to stop thinking that way.

"I guess we'll just part ways here then," she replied and pushed to her feet.

"I guess." He got up and brushed the dirt from the seat of his jeans. "Um, I'll see you around. I guess."

"Yup."

He'd taken maybe half a dozen steps back toward the horse trail that ran along the creek when she called out to him. "Hey, Rylan."

He turned and faced her, and the image of her standing in the twilight among the waving grass did something queer to his pulse.

"It was good to say my piece. Clear the air, so to speak."

"Good. It's probably better if we can be civil."

She nodded. "Well, see ya."

Kailey turned and started walking in the opposite direction, her hips swinging a little with each step, her towel and underwear balled up in her hand. Rylan looked down at the cotton in his hands and let out a huge breath before tucking his shorts half into his back pocket, the end trailing out like a handkerchief.

Civil. Clearing the air.

He was glad she was happy about it, because to his mind things just had gotten a whole lot more complicated.

Chapter 4

Kailey looked in the mirror and frowned. The dress fit perfectly. The boots were cute. Her hair was pulled back a little from the sides, but the curls were left in corkscrews over her bare shoulders. Thanks to Lacey's self-tanning cream, they'd managed to mostly blend her tan lines with her darker skin, though she could still tell where they were, particularly around her neck. Oh well. Hazards of being a farm girl and she wouldn't change that for anything.

Her makeup was perfect. The happy little bouquet of yellow and white flowers was on the bed behind her. Lacey was currently having her makeup done in the next room, and then Kailey would help her get dressed and calm the bride's frayed nerves.

There was a lot to do. A crazy day during a manic time of year for ranchers. There was no reason at all for her to be thinking about Rylan.

But she was.

All the damn time.

Now she was wondering what he'd think of her in this dress and hating herself for it. Was it wrong that she hoped it knocked out his eyeballs? It would serve him right...

And then there was that niggling knowledge that she wasn't entirely blameless in what had happened that night.

She turned away from the mirror and grabbed her bouquet. Might as well go to Lacey's room and focus on getting the bride ready for her big day rather than fret about what couldn't be changed.

She opened the door to the bedroom and nearly chucked her flowers as Rylan stood there, his fist poised to knock.

"What are you doing here?" she blurted out, and then let out the breath cramping her lungs. "Sorry. You just startled me."

"Quinn and Duke sent me over. I'm supposed to pick up Mom and David and take them to the church, then come back for you and Lacey."

"I thought Duke was going to do that."

His expression changed, as if he was trying to look nonchalant but was hiding something. "They ran into a slight snag. And that's all I'm going to say because I'm not equipped to deal with wedding-day drama. I'm to tell you that we're just saying that Duke is driving Quinn and Amber, and I'm driving you two like one big happy family."

He smiled at her. When he smiled at her that way she knew she'd agree to just about anything. She was such a weak woman where Rylan was concerned. Not that she'd tell him that. Like ever.

"Mum's the word. I don't know if Lacey is a nervous bride or not, but I'm not going to be the one to tempt fate." Worried, she looked fully into his face, trying to read it. "You're sure it's nothing major?"

"Major is relative on wedding days. Quinn's handling it. Don't you worry. By the time we get to the church, it'll be right as rain."

"I'm going to trust you."

"There's a first."

But the words were said in a teasing manner, not with an edge of sarcasm or hostility. She couldn't help it, she grinned back at him and in that shared moment she was reminded all over again why she'd found him attractive in the first place.

"I'm about to check on Lacey. You can go chill for a bit. We'll be ready soon."

He checked his watch. "Schedule says I need to have Mom to the church in twenty-five minutes. Can you tell her to meet me downstairs in fifteen?"

"Of course."

He turned to go back down the stairs and she got a good look at him. Black trousers and dress boots, a crisp white shirt and a tie. No jacket, but then he wasn't in the wedding party either, and it was June. He'd had his hair cut, the hint of dark auburn curls that were usually at his temples and neck clipped off in precise lines.

He was gorgeous—even if she did secretly prefer the bits of curl that added a roguish look to his rugged face.

"Ry?"

He turned around. "Yeah? Did you need something else?"

She shook her head. "N-no," she stammered. "I just wanted to say that, uh, you look nice today."

"So do you, K. So do you."

He threw her a wink and went down the stairs.

Kailey took a calming breath and opened the door to the master bedroom.

Lacey was sitting on a little stool in a lovely satin robe waiting to put on her gown. Her mom, Helen, was behind her, hooking a set of creamy pearls around Lacey's neck. Lacey had the Duggan coppery hair, and right now it was pulled back in a lovely romantic top knot with a simple circlet of white flowers around it.

"Is there a blushing bride in here somewhere?" Kailey asked, stepping inside.

God, Lacey looked happy. Her cheeks were flushed but not unnaturally. She was simply radiant, and calm, and so, so sweet looking. Helen couldn't stop smiling either. "We're nearly ready. Just the dress and boots to go."

"Kailey, you look beautiful. Thank you so much for doing this today."

"Of course I'd be here. Don't be silly." She put down her flowers and moved to the closet to get the dress. Together she and

Helen unzipped the garment bag and withdrew the soft material. Kailey draped it over her arm. "Okay, are you ready? I'll unzip and you step in."

It took no time at all for them to get Lacey zipped and hooked into the simple but stunning dress.

"Honey, you're beautiful."

"I know I said no to the whole veil thing, but you don't think white is, well, you know…"

Kailey gave a little snort. "That whole wearing white thing has been out the window for years. So what if this isn't your first trip down the aisle? We all know it's your last."

"Amen," Helen said, taking Lacey's hands in hers. "You've got a wonderful man in Quinn and a daughter to love now, too. I couldn't be prouder of you, sweetheart."

"Even though I'm here at the ranch?" Lacey looked troubled. "I know how you feel about the place, Mom."

"Ranch life wasn't for me, at least not without your father. But the nice thing about being an adult is being able to make your own choices. This is a good one. And I can tell because it's written all over your face."

Kailey's nose stung a little, the emotion of the day getting to her a bit as Lacey and Helen hugged. She wasn't sure if it was Carrie marrying Duke or Quinn finding Lacey or what, but Kailey had been chafing against her own life a little bit lately. Wanting more. Particularly since Colt had asked her that important question and then withdrawn it again once he'd understood how things would have to be.

She loved running the ranch with her dad. But she wanted her own life, too. Maybe... She bit down on her lip. Maybe even her own family. Colt had changed his mind because he'd wanted her to leave Gibson behind, and she couldn't bring herself to say goodbye to the ranch and the business her dad, and now she, had built. He'd wanted her to choose him. And for Kailey it just wasn't that simple.

But it had worked out for Quinn and Lacey, and Kailey was thrilled for them. "You just need your bouquet." Kailey went to the box containing the flowers and withdrew them from the tissue. "These are so pretty, Lacey. And, Helen, your corsage is in here, too. Maybe Lacey could pin it on you."

While Lacey did the honors, Kailey

snapped a few pictures with her phone that she'd send Lacey later. Then she handed Helen the boutonniere for David and let her know her ride was waiting to take them to the church.

It seemed in no time at all and Rylan was back to take them to the ceremony.

"Wait, I thought Duke was picking us up?" Lacey frowned at the sight of Rylan unfolding his legs as he got out of the car.

Kailey could tell that Lacey was getting nervous. There was no way she'd mention an emergency of any sort. Keeping Lacey calm and radiant was job number one, so she fudged a little. "I think it's nice. He doesn't have a part in the wedding, and I bet Quinn did it so Rylan would be involved, you know?"

"Do you think?" Lacey looked so pleased that Kailey knew she'd taken the right tack.

Kailey couldn't take her eyes off him. "Sure I do. Now your whole family has a role to play in your big day."

Rylan had borrowed Helen and David's sedan for the occasion, so that Lacey didn't have to get in and out of a half-ton truck in her gown. Sunglasses shaded his eyes as he held the car door, first for Lacey, and then the other side for Kailey, once she had finished tucking the mini-train in around Lacey's ankles.

"Forget what I said about you looking nice," he said in a low voice, his hands resting on the window. "You look beautiful, Kailey. Really, really beautiful."

Surprise and pleasure had her throat tightening. "Thank you, Rylan," she murmured.

"You're welcome," he answered. Then he shut the door behind her and went around to the driver's side as if he'd done nothing more important than comment on the weather. The compliment had gone straight to her heart, though, because she knew it had been sincere.

It was a perfect day for a wedding. The early summer sun was warm but not too hot, and a light breeze ruffled the hems of their dresses as they got out of the car at the church. Duke was there, holding Amber's hand. Kailey grinned when she saw Amber's face. She was as proud as anything in her white flower-girl dress with a sash that matched the color of Kailey's. A little basket was in her hands, and once more, the brown-and-blue boots on her feet. She was adorable. Even more so when she ran forward, pulling her hand out of Duke's grasp.

"Lacey! You look like a princess!"

Ignoring her hem, Lacey squatted down to Amber's height. "So do you, pumpkin. You ready to do this?"

"Heck yeah."

Kailey burst out laughing at the slightly inappropriate answer from a five-year-old. Confused, Amber looked up, but then Duke bade them goodbye as he went to meet Quinn at the front of the church, and Rylan sent her one parting look before giving his arm to Carrie—they'd sit together with Helen and David throughout the service.

They were waiting in the vestibule, nearly ready for the walk up the aisle when Lacey spoke. "Amber, do I have bride brain? I thought we got you a yellow and white bouquet like Kailey's. Not a basket."

Amber turned troubled eyes on her nearly new stepmother. "Oh. Um. Well."

"Um well?"

"Molly and Ranger ate them."

The dogs. Quinn had taken both puppies to his house so that they'd be away from the bridal trappings. But apparently flower-girl flowers weren't immune to their antics.

"They what?" Lacey's expression was horrified.

Amber's lip quivered. "I'm sorry. I just put them down for a minute. Daddy put the dogs on the porch and Uncle Duke went to the store. That's why Uncle Rylan came to get you. Duke was getting me new flowers."

Lacey raised an eyebrow in Kailey's direction and Kailey tried to adopt an innocent look. "I see," she said, and Kailey shrugged.

"I think they're pretty," Amber continued. "Don't you like them, Lacey?" Her big eyes were worried.

Kailey had to admit that they were lovely. For a rush job, the sunflowers, daisies and baby's breath were a pretty close match to the other bouquets.

Lacey smiled down at Amber. "Don't worry. I think they're very pretty. Maybe prettier than the ones we ordered. Now, are you ready for your walk up the aisle?"

Amber nodded. "Lacey, I'm glad you're going to be my new mommy." She wrapped her arms around Lacey's hips for a quick hug, and Kailey saw Lacey's eyes mist over.

Moments later Kailey watched from the front of the church as Lacey walked down the aisle to where Quinn was waiting. For the first ten steps she had her gaze locked on Lacey, looking so happy and stunning in her dress. But then she looked at Quinn and her heart turned over. He was watching his bride walk toward him with pure, naked adoration written all over his face. She'd seen him happy with his first wife, Marie, had seen him devastated when Marie died. No one she knew deserved a second chance at happiness more than Quinn.

But more than that, she wondered if anyone would ever look at her that way. As if she was the entire world. As if she was the sun that brought all the light and warmth to his life. Because that was exactly how Quinn was looking at Lacey. And for the first time, Kailey wanted that for herself.

She wanted to matter. She wanted to be more than Kailey Brandt, rancher. Kailey Brandt, friend.

She wanted to be Kailey Brandt, *everything*.

She turned and focused on the minister and what he was saying as the ceremony got under way. And she definitely didn't sneak looks at Rylan, sitting with a very pregnant Carrie in the second pew. Because Rylan

Duggan was the last man on earth who would ever want her to be that person.

The reception was held at a golf course just north of town. Tents were set up outside the club house, and guests mingled around sipping punch and nibbling on snacks as the wedding party arrived after pictures. Kailey hadn't minded the photos much. The photographer had been efficient and funny, and in no time at all they'd been on their way. Now they were at the country club where there'd be a sit-down dinner and a dance. It still all added up to a long day.

She was already tired. Haying would start in a few days if the weather held. What she really wanted to do now was get out of this dress, put on some pajamas and get a good night's sleep.

The bride and groom began mingling with the guests in the minutes before the meal was served, and Kailey found herself at the punch bowl, filling a cup and hoping the cool drink and sugar hit might perk her up. She'd taken a cautious sip when Rylan came up behind her.

"Is it any good?"

She looked up at him. "Is it very bad of

me to say it would be improved by a shot of vodka?"

He chuckled, his gaze warm. "You look like you've put in a full day. Everything okay?"

She nodded. "I swear, I could spend a whole day working on the ranch and not find it as exhausting as this."

"Who knew getting pretty could be so tiring, huh?"

She made a face at him. "Smart aleck."

Rylan poured himself some punch. "It's a crazy time to have a wedding, but I don't think they wanted to wait. It all came together pretty fast."

"Don't I know it." She smiled a little. "And I'm happy for them. You didn't know Quinn before, but he's had a rough time. They're good for each other."

"How come you've never gotten hitched?" They'd moved away from the punch bowl and were now ambling around the fresh-cut grass. The scent of blossoms from the tidy flower beds perfumed the air.

"Me?" She tossed him what she hoped was a saucy grin. "Why, sir, no one would have me." Despite the light tone, it was the absolute truth.

"I'm surprised."

And that surprised her. "You are?"

"Sure," he replied. "You're pretty, smart, strong and successful..."

"Gee, Rylan. I never knew you thought so much of me." She couldn't resist teasing him a little. Things *had* been a little easier since their talk at the swimming hole. Not that she didn't still notice him. A blind woman would notice those bedroom eyes and that muscled body. But their chat had cleared the air considerably. They both knew what and what not to expect.

"I take it back. I know why you haven't been asked."

"Why?" Intrigued, she stopped and looked up at him.

"Because you're pretty, smart, strong and successful. I bet most of the guys around here are intimidated as hell. You make them look bad, sugar."

Her temper flared so quickly she wondered if puffs of steam were coming out of her ears. "So, what, I should dumb myself down to snag a husband?" Or perhaps abandon the business she'd put her heart and soul into so her husband's pride wouldn't take a dent?

Hmm. Maybe it wasn't really Rylan she was mad at. Maybe she was still furious with Colt for giving her such a ridiculous ultimatum.

Rylan looked appropriately horrified, and his lips twitched as he tried not to laugh. "Absolutely not. You keep those standards right up high where they belong." He lifted his hand and twined a finger inside one of her long ringlets. "You need someone who's able to go toe-to-toe with you, Curly. Or else you'll be bored to death."

Funny how she seemed to go toe-to-toe, as he put it, with him quite regularly. But he was not the man for her. Rylan Duggan went where the wind blew him and certainly wasn't looking to be tied down.

She stepped back, aware that she could get sucked into his charm without a whole lot of effort on his part. "There's something to be said for boredom," she replied tartly. "At least you know where you stand."

Damn man, he just grinned at her, his blue eyes sparkling. "Touché."

"Maybe we should talk about something else."

"Good idea. I think Crooked Valley needs a stud."

She coughed, felt the sting of the punch in her nose. She bent over a little and her eyes watered as she had the unholy urge to laugh. Why was it he seemed to be able to do that to her without even trying? A napkin appeared in front of her face and she took it, dabbed her lips and eyes, the whole time aware that Rylan was standing there with a smirk on his too-handsome face.

"You did that on purpose," she accused.

"Maybe. But I am serious, you know. Can you breathe now? Everything okay?"

"Besides you driving me nuts? Perfectly fine." She offered an angelic smile. With teeth.

"Okay, so back to business. I've been thinking about what you said a few weeks back at the diner."

"About your program."

He nodded, and she noticed he looked semi-serious now. Rylan pretty much always looked as if he were privy to some sort of inside joke, but she was starting to realize it was just who he was. Part of his innate charisma.

"We've got some solid stock, but nothing spectacular, nothing that's creating any buzz or fuss. Not like you. You've built up your breeding program so that you've got some great bloodlines running through yours. It's been smart."

"You've checked?"

"Of course I have." As if oblivious to her surprise, he continued on. "Crooked Valley doesn't have that. According to Quinn, about five years ago Joe took it in his head to *dabble* with the idea."

"Yeah. He came to my dad for advice."

"And he made a decent start, I'll give him that. But it's not growing and it needs to. Right now it's costing Crooked Valley far more than it's making."

She agreed with him. "But where are you going to get this stud savior?" she asked. "I can't see Duke signing off on that kind of purchase. To get what you're looking for... we're talking a minimum of ten grand. Probably more like fifteen or twenty."

"I'm working on that. I guess my question to you is would Brandt consider using our stud in your program? If we had one?"

She stopped and looked up at him. He was dead serious now. Was he really taking that big of an interest in the ranch? How much did he have at stake?

It was easier to talk to him with her work

hat on. "Rylan, you know as well as I do that it would depend on the horse, and what you'd charge."

"But if you did like what you saw, you'd consider it?"

"I consider everything."

"That's all I needed to know."

The guests were called to dinner then, and Kailey and Rylan parted ways. He sat with his parents and Quinn's mother while Duke, Carrie and Kailey sat with Quinn, Lacey and Amber. Throughout the meal Kailey thought about what Rylan had said about Crooked Valley. He didn't talk like a man who wasn't invested. Instead, it sounded very much like planning for the future.

Then again, he was one-third owner, at least technically. She supposed making the bucking stock operation profitable would pad his bottom line, too. Help fund his expenses. She'd seen his results. The NFR was a definite possibility this year if he kept on the way he'd begun. Shoot, he'd said that he'd been in the money on the last rodeo. He didn't say that he'd won top spot. She'd only seen that when she'd checked the standings.

She looked over at him, saw him laugh at something Quinn's mother said. Something in her heart softened. This wouldn't do, not at all. She couldn't be starting to like him. Not after he'd been such a jerk.

Which he'd apologized for. Sincerely.

Maybe she should be better at holding grudges.

After dinner the tables were cleared to make room for the dancing to come later. Lacey and Quinn cut the cake and fed each other while people snapped pictures. The band tuned up and they had the first dance, then David danced with Lacey while Quinn danced with his mother, and then Lacey danced with Duke while Quinn danced with Helen. Once the family dances were out of the way, Kailey was called upon to dance with Duke. Finally the slow songs ended and the band sped up for some boot stomping music. Kailey wondered how much longer she had to stay.

Then she felt guilty for wanting to leave. How often did she get to dress up and party? A year ago, heck, even six months ago, she would have really cut loose at something like this. Danced until last call.

At some point she'd changed. Decided life should hold more meaning than the daily grind. She'd...grown up. Problem was, she hadn't yet found that extra meaning and it seemed as if there was a big hole where it was supposed to be.

It was around the time that Lacey was going to throw the bouquet that Kailey realized she hadn't seen Rylan in a while. The girlfriend of one of the ranch hands caught the flowers, and the evening began to fade into purply twilight. Still no Rylan. Had he gone home?

She finally caught up with Lacey at the bar, where her friend was ordering a plain tonic water with lime. "Hey, Lace, have you seen Rylan?"

Lacey took a sip of her drink and fanned her face, which was pink with the exertion of dancing. "He left."

"Left?" Now why on earth should she be feeling disappointed? Still, he just up and took off from his sister's wedding?

"Quinn's mom wasn't feeling so well, and Amber was getting tired. Duke was going to take them back to Great Falls, but Carrie…" Lacey grinned. "I think they're just Braxton Hicks contractions, but she's a bit worried with a bit over a month left to go, and Duke was getting on her case about overdoing the dancing. Rylan offered to drive instead."

"Oh. That was nice of him."

"It was. You know, Kailey, I'm not excusing his behavior before. But he really is a decent guy. He didn't have to come back here at all. He did it for Duke and he did it for me. He won't admit it, but in his way he's trying to help. I really do believe that."

"Me, too," she admitted.

"You do?" Lacey sipped on her straw, her eyebrows lifting at Kailey's unexpected agreement.

"We've talked about bucking stock a few times. He might not stick around, but I get the sense he does actually care what happens to the place. I think he'll do what he needs to so you and Duke can keep it."

Kailey got a glass of ice water from a pitcher to the side of the bar and Lacey followed her there. "You know he was like that when we were kids, too."

"Like what?" She tried to picture Rylan as a child. It wasn't that hard. Hair a little lighter—perhaps a true redhead—and with a devilish twinkle in his eye.

"Devil-may-care, like nothing mattered. Things rolled off him like water off a duck's back. But when the chips were down, he'd come through. Like the year I lost my purse when we were Christmas shopping. I'd saved my allowance for weeks to be able to buy presents for Mom and him and Duke. I was probably ten years old. Duke gave me a lecture on responsibility. Rylan reached into his wallet and gave me half his money, which was more than I'd had to begin with."

"How sweet."

"He really was." Lacey smiled with fondness. "We kind of thought he'd outgrow his fascination with rodeo as he got older. Instead, he graduated high school and took off the next day. Found a job, then another, started competing and ended up at a big place in Wyoming."

"And now here."

Lacey nodded. "I don't pretend to understand him. I understood Duke's need to follow in our dad's footsteps with the military. And me…" Her face softened a little. "I just wanted a home and family with a mom and a dad and a perfect little life."

"And you got it."

"I do now." Her smile was beautiful. "But I've never quite understood what drives Rylan. He just goes from place to place like he's searching for something."

"Or running away."

"Or that. Either way, I'm enjoying spending more time with him. I'll take it for as long as it lasts."

Quinn came over to claim his bride for a dance. "Are you ready to leave soon?" he asked. Kailey felt that little bit of longing in the pit of her stomach again. Clearly Quinn couldn't wait to begin married life with his bride.

She hated that she was jealous.

Lacey gave Kailey a quick hug. "Looks like we're heading out in a bit. I just want to say thank you, for everything. It's been a perfect day."

"Yes, it has," Kailey agreed.

She stayed until they drove away in Lacey's car, headed to a resort in the mountains for a few days of privacy and an abbreviated honeymoon. It wasn't until they were gone that Kailey realized she'd been left without a ride back to the ranch, where her truck was parked. Duke had taken Carrie home, being the concerned dad-to-be. Once more she chafed against circumstances; she was going to have to ask her parents to give her a lift.

Maybe it was finally time for her to find a place of her own. On her own.

Chapter 5

The porch light was off and the house was dark when Kailey retrieved the spare key from under a flower pot and let herself in. Her jeans and T-shirt were upstairs, along with her makeup bag and curling iron. She'd grab them and head home and to bed. Tomorrow was Sunday, but there were still chores to be done.

She was halfway down the stairs when she heard the front door open.

"Duke? That you?"

Footsteps paused. "Kailey?"

It was Rylan. Damn.

"I just came back to get my stuff. And my

truck." She went the rest of the way down the stairs. She could do this. It didn't matter that they were alone. It changed nothing.

And then she turned the corner and saw him standing in the kitchen, still in his wedding clothes but with his tie untied and hanging around his neck, the top buttons of his shirt undone.

Trouble. Times ten and then some.

"I just got back. Came in for a beer before heading to bed. You want one?"

"I've got to drive home."

He didn't argue with her or make a smart comment like "you don't have to." She appreciated that. It was the sort of thing he might have said a few months ago. In fact, she was pretty sure it was close to verbatim what he'd said at the Valentine's Day dance.

"Do you want something else? Ginger ale? I think I saw some of that in the fridge."

Actually, it sounded good. "Sure. I guess."

He reached in and got a can, handed it to her without the benefit of a glass. She popped the top and watched as he opened his beer. "Want to sit on the porch for a few minutes?" she suggested. It would be better than staring at each other here in the kitchen. "I could stand a few minutes of peace and quiet."

They made their way outside to the veranda, settled into the deep wooden chairs that lived there during the summer months. Kailey let out a sigh. "It's nice to sit. In the stillness, I mean." She could still hear peepers chirping from the ditches, and a cool breeze fluttered the leaves on the trees. Up on the porch, though, they were sheltered from the wind.

"I thought you liked music and commotion."

"I do. I don't know why, but I was just tired today." Dissatisfied, really, she realized. And had been for a while now.

Silence stretched out.

"It was nice of you to take Mrs. Solomon home."

He took a long pull of his beer. "It was no biggie. It was a long day for her. Plus Amber was getting tired. She fell asleep on the drive."

"She sure looked cute in her flower-girl dress."

"Yes," he said, his voice deep and smooth. "She sure did."

Kailey had just taken a long, cool drink

of ginger ale when Rylan added, "And you looked pretty, too, Kailey. That color suits you."

She was still wearing her dress. She'd figured she'd jump in the truck, head home, maybe take a bath before bed. "Lacey chose it," she said, and somehow her voice sounded strangled in the peaceful night.

This was probably a mistake. Right now all she was picturing was the sight of him changing back into his jeans after swimming, his body corded and muscled and the scar on his left hip from a long-ago injury. She should leave. Take her bag and get in her truck and go as quickly as possible. He was no good for her.

Yet she couldn't seem to make herself get out of her chair.

He was right beside her, close enough that she could smell his aftershave, sense the warmth of his body. Her right leg was crossed over her left knee, and she watched, transfixed, as Rylan reached over and touched the skin just below her hem with a single finger. Her eyes fluttered closed as all her senses went on high alert. Warning bells crashed through her brain, but she didn't hear them. She was so focused on the delicious feel of that single finger lightly grazing the skin right above her knee. No higher or lower. Just back and forth, a lazy caress, sending her hormones into overdrive.

"Ry," she whispered, a warning wrapped in a sigh.

"I know," he answered softly. "I know I shouldn't. But you're so damned pretty."

She swallowed against the lump in her throat.

"I can't seem to stay away from you," he lamented, all the while the rough pad of his finger slid back and forth on her skin. "I know I should. I know I'm not the kind of man you want. Hell, I don't want to be. And yet here I am, wondering if I dare kiss you again."

How was it that one innocent touch could send her body into a nuclear meltdown?

"Why'd you have to come back, anyway?" She closed her eyes, losing herself to the sensation of being seduced. By his voice, by his touch, by simply being here in the dark with him.

"I ask myself that a million times a day," he answered, and now it was his hand on her knee, sliding beneath the light fabric of her dress, running over her thigh. "I don't know, Kailey. I just don't know."

"Me either," she said, and opened her eyes. Her whole body was at attention. "Ry, you either have to stop or kiss me because I'm dying over here."

It was all she had to say. Slowly, so slowly it was sweet torture, Ry slipped his hand away from her leg and pushed himself up out of the deck chair. Then he leaned over her, his hands braced against the arms of her chair, and touched her lips with his.

This was what she remembered. What she'd hungered for. The memory had been accurate but not nearly as good as the reality, and she put her hands on his shoulders, kissed him back. When he lowered himself farther, kneeling in front of her chair, something flashed through her mind, a remembrance of how good, how intense, how consuming it had been making love to him. They wouldn't go that far tonight. Couldn't. But she'd waited three and a half long months to touch him again.

He let go of the chair and put his hands on her hips, pulling her forward a little so that her legs parted and he knelt between them. She leaned forward and kissed him back,

his head just slightly below hers. A gasp
sounded in the stillness—hers—when his
lips slid away and trailed down her neck to
the hollow of her throat.

Yet something didn't feel right. It wasn't
even the way he'd left her before that was
sticking in the back of her mind somewhere. It was the knowledge that he'd leave
her again. And recognizing that, at least for
her, there was more at work than sexual attraction.

He was fun, he was charming. He cared
for his brother and sister and was good with
kids. If they played with the fire that was desire, she would be the one who got burned
the worst.

"Stop," she breathed, torn between knowing they had to cease this craziness and
never wanting it to end. "We can't do this,
Ry. We can't."

"We already are," he murmured, his
tongue sliding behind her ear and sending
shivers down her spine.

"No." She put her hands on his arms and
gripped them firmly, pushing him away. "I
don't want this."

He stopped, but he met her gaze boldly.

"You're a liar. You do want it. You want it as much as I do, Kailey."

Damn him for making things so difficult. "Yes. I do. Physically. But it's more than that for me, and it'll never be more than that for you. Do you understand?"

He frowned. "You make it sound like I don't care about you at all."

Kailey sighed, wished he'd move so she didn't feel pinned in her chair. But at least he'd stopped, moved back so that he wasn't right in her space anymore.

How could she explain that everything had changed the morning she'd woken alone, without making him think that she was in love with him? She wasn't. But it had been the kick in the pants she needed. A cold-water slap of reality.

"Ry, neither of us can deny that there's a certain…attraction between us. But something changed in February, the morning I woke up and you were gone."

She met his gaze, hoped she wasn't blushing. Confession and unloading her feelings wasn't really her style. "It was a wake-up call to me. I know what I want, and it's not what you want, and I'd only be setting myself up to get hurt."

He finally sat back on his heels. "Jeez, Kailey."

"Ry, you're not a bad guy. You're funny and charming and fairly kind. You'd have the power to hurt me, and I can't walk into that. This really isn't about me being angry about what happened then. It's more... understanding what would surely happen now, and being smart enough to avoid it."

Rylan sat down on his rump and pushed back the few extra inches until his back rested against the veranda railing. "You know, in my experience most women see that as a challenge. That I'm a project that needs to be fixed."

Kailey understood that, too. Heck, she'd been there. Attracted to the unattainable guy, so sure that she was the one who could change his mind and tame his bad-boy ways. Colt Black had been a prime example. She'd taken her time, certain he'd come around and reconsider, and then he'd found someone else. On Valentine's Day she'd started dancing with Rylan just to make Colt jealous. Make him see what he'd given up...

"I'm not interested in fixing anyone." She let out a sigh and then a little laugh. "Shoot, do you think this means I'm getting old?"

He chuckled a little, too. "Not old. Wise." He held her gaze, his eyes nearly black in the moonlit evening. "Look, I'm not going to deny that I'm disappointed. You do something to me, Kailey. But I also appreciate you shooting straight with me."

"I don't want to be angry at you," she replied. "I just want…"

That was just it. Part of her still wanted to throw caution to the wind and fall into his arms. The other part wanted them to find a way to coexist for the next few months until he left Crooked Valley behind.

"I just want us to be friends. Do you think that's even possible?"

"I don't see why not."

"Okay. Good." Yet agreeing to keep things 100 percent platonic caused an awkward silence to fall over the evening. "I'd better go. Mom and Dad will be wondering where I am."

He grinned and she rolled her eyes. "I know. Don't say it. I'm too old to live with my parents."

"No judgment," he replied, the smile still on his face.

"Cool." She got up and went inside to get her bag. When she came back out, Rylan was still sitting with his back against the veranda railing, his arms resting on his knees. He looked a little sexy and a little bit sad at the same time. Definitely lonely.

She looped her keys over her index finger and went down the steps, her boots sounding extra loud in the stillness of the night. She paused at the bottom and looked back up at him.

"Rylan? For some reason, you seem to sell yourself short. Maybe if you stopped doing that, you wouldn't feel the need to keep running."

He spun to look at her, and she shrugged. "Just a suggestion."

She drove back to the ranch, her body still humming from his touch, but sure in her head that she'd done the right thing.

It was just unfortunate that her heart took a little more convincing.

This time when Rylan rolled into Crooked Valley, it was midafternoon and he was pulling a horse trailer behind him. The latest rodeo had taken him north, and he'd come out on top again. The side trip he'd made yesterday had turned out to be worth it, and the prize money had come in handy.

Very handy. He whistled as he pulled up next to the corral outside the horse barn and carefully backed the trailer toward the gate.

He parked and hopped out, then checked the doors and gates to make sure the corral was secure. Only then did he swing open the gate behind his trailer and prepare to let out Rattler, the newest addition to the Crooked Valley stock contracting business.

He could hear the stomps and crashes of hooves in the back and he grinned. This stallion was full of piss and vinegar for sure. Getting him into the trailer had been interesting, but Rylan knew how to be patient. Just as he'd be patient now.

Rattler could be a pussycat if he wanted to. At least with no one trying to sit on his back.

Randy, one of the hands who worked mostly with the horses, came out of the barn and ambled up to the fence. "Whatcha got in the trailer, Ry?"

"A present. Do me a favor and stand over here, will ya, Randy? I'm going to let him out."

A thump echoed against the side of the trailer. "Sounds like a bruiser," Randy mused.

"We'll find out when I get him in the chute," Rylan answered. He was pretty sure he'd made a sound investment. And even Duke couldn't argue about the price because Rylan had a plan for that, too. Just because his plans didn't include sticking around in the long term didn't mean he couldn't help invest in the ranch's future.

"Ready?"

Rattler thundered out of the trailer with a clatter of angry hooves, charging down the ramp and straight through into the corral. He was off like a shot, kicking up his legs in a tantrum-like statement. The equivalent, Rylan figured, of giving him the finger for keeping him closed up for so long. He chuckled, impressed and, to his surprise, quite excited. Rattler could make all the difference to Crooked Valley if Duke could hang tight for the investment to pay off.

"He's a pretty one." Randy nodded.

"Don't let him hear you say that. You'll offend his manhood." But he was secretly inclined to agree. "Close the gate, Randy. I'm going to pull the trailer ahead."

By the time he'd moved the truck, a small crowd had gathered by the fence. Carrie had come down from the house, bringing

Lacey with her. Duke and Quinn came into the yard as supper time drew close. Unconcerned, Rattler trotted around the fenced circle, his mane streaming and eyes bright.

"What in the world?" Duke asked, a deep frown marring his face.

"Meet Rattler, the newest stud for your bucking stock." Rylan kept his voice deliberately upbeat and light.

"My what?"

Duke looked anything but pleased, and Rylan saw him exchange a look with Carrie. A look that set Rylan's teeth on edge. *Uh-oh*, it said. *What's Rylan gone and done now?*

"Rylan. Where on earth did you get this horse?"

"At Mack Rigden's place outside Dickinson. Mack's thinking about retiring soon. I heard a rumor that he was going to take some stock to auction, so I made a detour on the way home."

"Why on earth… Did it occur to you to run this past me? Or Quinn?"

Rylan held his cool. He'd expected some resistance, after all. "We all know what you need to keep the program going is a good sire. One that others will pay stud fees for."

"And it'll take a long damn time for him

to earn his keep! What were you thinking, doing this without consulting me? Forget upkeep, there's no way we could afford this right now."

He'd expected Duke to be mad. He looked at Lacey and saw hope on her face. Things didn't really change, did they? Duke was the oldest and figured he should have the final word on everything. And Lacey was the tenderhearted one who believed in him even when she shouldn't.

He hated the thought of letting them down. He'd avoided putting himself in this position for a lot of years. He'd hated the idea of coming back here, facing all the old hurts, irritated that Grandpa Joe was yanking them around like puppets on a string even after his death. If he had to be here, he was going to do it his way. At least some of the time, anyway.

"I knew what you'd say."

"For Pete's sake, Ry. Lacey's been trying to trim some costs since she came on, and we've both got families to support."

Ouch.

"Duke," Carrie admonished quietly.

But Duke was well and truly irritated. "Well, it's true. Rylan's been going wherever the wind takes him without a care in the world, and now Lacey and I both depend on this ranch to support our spouses and children. Meanwhile, he can blow in like a tornado and leave again just as quickly."

Ry's temper flared, and he struggled to measure his words. He didn't ask for this. He was trying to help, for God's sake. But clearly his brother had some issues he needed to get off his chest.

"Crooked Valley isn't on the hook for a red cent, so don't get your panties in a twist." Ry lifted his chin. "Rattler's mine. I bought him with my own money."

Duke's jaw dropped. Lacey stared. "Your own money?" she asked. "But, Ry, you said before that a good stud horse would be expensive."

"How expensive?" Duke asked, an edge to his voice.

Carrie and Quinn remained silent, as if sensing this was between the siblings.

"Seventeen and a half."

Duke cursed. Carrie's eyes widened. Even Quinn let out a low whistle.

"You're going to ask, so I'll save you the trouble. I've had a good year. And I've been working for years. My last place, my board was covered in the winter and in the summer I stayed in the RV. My only expenses were my truck and the clothes on my back. I managed to put some away. Then when I sold the camper and bought the smaller one I still had money in the bank."

Not only in the bank. He'd never been much of a spender, kept things simple rather than extravagant. He'd actually taken the step of investing some of his salary every payday. If he told them how much, they'd never believe him. He wasn't even thirty yet and he had a nice little nest egg.

Duke ran his hand through his hair. "You should have come to me. We should have talked about it."

"I was trying to do something good here. The opportunity came up and I seized it. Yeah, I paid a good price for him, but I would have been on the hook for more if I'd waited for him to go to auction."

The fire in Duke's eyes was starting to mellow.

"Look, Duke, here's the deal. For all intents and purposes, Rattler is part of Crooked Valley. We can use him to breed our mares. He'll earn his keep with breeding fees. He's going to be in demand, I promise you. And all the money will go into ranch coffers. The only thing I ask is that his ownership stays with me."

It felt like a big step. Owning Rattler tied him to Crooked Valley in a bigger way than he cared to be, but he also knew it was the only way Duke would agree to the purchase.

"I don't know, Ry."

"Trust me," he entreated. "I've been doing this a long time, Duke. Hell, if you don't trust my judgment, trust Kailey's. Have her come over and give her opinion."

He thought about it for a moment and took it a step further. "I'll make you a deal. If Kailey comes over and says I made a mistake, I'll take him to auction."

He looked at all of them. Quinn's gaze held a glimmer of respect and even Duke looked uncomfortably resigned to the idea. It was an impulsive suggestion, and things were hot and cold with Kailey, depending on the situation. But he trusted her horse sense. Brandt's stock was top-notch. He also trusted her to be honest—even if she didn't like it.

Hmm. It had been quite a while since he'd really trusted anyone that much. And that included Duke and Lacey.

Quinn stepped forward. "I think that's a fair idea, Rylan. Kailey's been helpful with advice for me over the past several months and there's no question she knows what she's doing. What do you say, Duke?"

Duke gave a short nod. "I'll agree to that. I'll hear what she has to say before making any decisions."

Rylan bit his tongue, knowing he had to choose his moments. And he realized that Duke had taken on the bulk of the day-to-day operations of the ranch. But, dammit, they each owned a third. They each had equal say. He looked over at Lacey, who was now looking uncomfortable, probably because she was caught in the middle. He knew if it came down to it, she'd go with whatever Duke wanted. Duke, the natural leader. Not Rylan, the baby of the family.

Meanwhile, Ry went to the truck and retrieved an apple from a bag he had on the seat. He applied just the right pressure to break it in half, and he took a bite, crunching into the white flesh while holding the other half on the palm of his hand.

All he had to do was hold his hand over the top of the fence for about two seconds and Rattler started trotting over. Hide glistening and eyes bright, he lipped the fruit from Ry's palm and chewed contentedly, bits of apple and juice flying.

"Atta boy," Ry soothed quietly, rubbing his hand along Rattler's neck. "The ladies are gonna love you."

Quinn interrupted the moment. "Kailey says she can come over after supper."

"Thanks, Quinn," Ry said. He got the sense that Quinn was an ally and was actually relieved someone had stepped up with the stock program. But maybe the ranch manager wasn't saying much because he didn't want to put himself in the middle of a family issue. Couldn't hate a guy for that.

While Quinn and Duke went to do evening chores, Carrie and Lacey headed to the house. Ry stayed behind, watching Rattler become accustomed to his new surroundings. There was a particularly big stall at the near end of the barn that he could claim, though for right now what the stallion really needed was to be turned out to pasture. That was something Ry would have to talk to Quinn about, since they had a number of open mares and the last thing Ry wanted to happen was some unplanned breeding.

He skipped the family dinner and instead parked the trailer, cleaned it out and unloaded his stuff in the camper. Then he went back out and took a good look at the brood mares. If Kailey was on board, if he could get her to hold true to her promise to use a new stud for Brandt's stock, it would be a big boost for Crooked Valley's reputation.

He'd like to breed one or two of their own mares, too. Like Candyfloss, an Appaloosa with some Clyde blood in her. She had a size and attitude that Rylan liked to see in a horse. Manageable and friendly when not in the chute, but a natural bucking instinct that he thought would work well with Rattler's temperament. With her strength and Rattler's high spirits, he figured there was a chance of breeding a good saddle bronc.

After Rylan had gone through the barn, he went back to the corral and leaned on the fence, watching as Rattler stood in the sun, his hide twitching now and again.

And swallowed against a lump in his throat.

When he'd been little, he'd loved this ranch. He'd loved the horses and the cows and Grandma Eileen's cooking. He'd wanted to run through the fields and pastures all day long, climb on the huge, round bales of hay, pick up garter snakes in the grass. He'd ridden his pony every opportunity he'd had, and when he wasn't doing that he'd nagged Duke to play rodeo with him. It usually had involved lassoes and some sort of mock calf Grandpa Joe had set up for them behind the barn. Duke, if Rylan remembered correctly, had done it grudgingly. At first Ry had thought it was because Duke didn't want to be saddled with a younger brother. But now, Rylan realized something important: Duke had always wanted to be a soldier. Out of all the kids, it had been Rylan who'd missed the ranch the most.

When they'd moved to Helena, Rylan hadn't fit in anywhere. In his ideal world, he was back on the ranch, with the horses and the cattle, currying Daisy's coat and feeding her carrots. Not in a city school where kids teased him if he wore his boots and hat. Even the week or so in the summer that they'd used to visit hadn't been fun, because it only served to remind Rylan that he had to say goodbye and go back to the city he'd hated.

Rattler wandered around the corral and Rylan sighed. He'd put off coming back here because it hurt too much. Because he resented being ripped away from it in the first place. He wished it didn't feel so much like home again. Wished he could stay detached. But he knew that his biggest fear had already come to pass.

He was going to hate leaving again.

Chapter 6

Kailey thought about taking her truck over to Crooked Valley, but it was too nice of a night. She was bone-tired from haying all day, but the before-supper shower had felt heavenly and the beef roast and mashed potatoes her mom had made for dinner had perked her up considerably. What she really wanted was to enjoy some peace and quiet rather than feel rushed from place to place. She saddled one of the geldings and went cross-country in the soft evening, the rhythm of being on horseback soothing and familiar and far preferable to sitting on tractors all day long.

Rylan was standing at the corral, his elbows on the fence. He didn't seem to hear her approach, and she frowned. He was usually quick to smile, but right now his body language suggested he was lost in thought. Tough thoughts. His shoulders hunched and his head drooped a little as he rested his weight on the fence rail.

"Hey, Duggan," she called out, realizing she'd assessed the situation accurately when he jumped in surprise.

"I was looking for your truck," he said, flashing a smile that erased the troubled expression from his face. Whatever thoughts had been dogging him, he'd pushed them aside. She was starting to realize he was very good at that.

"This was more relaxing. I've been haying all day."

"I just got back this afternoon."

She dismounted and tied her horse to a nearby fence post. "So I heard," she answered, crossing the yard, moving toward him. "Caused quite a hubbub with your cargo, too."

His gaze warmed. "Come see."

She stood beside him at the fence and gave a whistle. The horse's ears perked up at the sound and he turned his head. He sure was a beauty. Heavily muscled, strong hind-quarters, broad chest and standing seventeen hands or more if she was any judge.

"He can buck?"

"I certainly hope so." Together they watched as the horse caught wind of something and lifted his head before trotting to the opposite side of the corral. "Previous owner retired him from competition a few years back. He was becoming valuable from a breeding standpoint."

"And he sold him why?"

"Retiring. You probably know him. Mack Rigden."

"I know Mack. Good guy." She narrowed her eyes. "He selling off more of his stock?"

Rylan laughed then. "You interested?"

"If they look anything like this big lad, I might be." She hesitated. "I'd have to look at the bloodline, but I'd say there's a little draft horse in there somewhere. Percheron, maybe. You breed him with Candy and you'll have a horse like a tank."

He chuckled. "I was thinking the same thing."

Kailey kept her eyes on the stallion as she pondered the question on her mind. "Ry, I don't know how to ask this delicately, so I'll just come out with it. I didn't think Duke would approve an expenditure this big. Not now. What changed his mind?"

"He didn't change his mind. That's why Quinn called you."

Her face must have looked shocked because Rylan started to laugh. "You should see yourself," he joked. "You look horrified. Don't worry, Kailey. I didn't rip off Crooked Valley funds. I paid for him myself."

She thought about that for a moment. First of all, there was the surprise that he had enough money for a really good stud horse when he was living out of a tiny camper. More than that, though, she thought about how this marked an interesting step in his involvement at Crooked Valley.

So much for no ties. He had the horse. He had already mentioned one potential pairing. Did he realize he'd just made an investment in the family bucking stock business?

"I take it you live below your means, then," she said quietly, resting her arms on the fence.

"Not hard to do. My needs are pretty simple."

She looked over at him, surprised. This

was a different side to Rylan she hadn't seen before. She'd always had the impression he didn't take things very seriously. That he was…impulsive. Despite what Duke might have thought, this wasn't an impulsive purchase.

He'd asked her before what she thought. Asked if she'd consider helping him out. He'd been planning this. Looking for the right horse. He'd had money put aside.

It was completely opposite from the man who'd thrown his cash down for a custom-made saddle at the Valentine's Day auction, who'd danced with her and propositioned her to something outrageous…

"Who are you, Rylan?"

She didn't realize she'd asked the question out loud until she heard him sigh. "I just am," he answered, avoiding the question. "No sense trying to dig too deep with me. What you see is what you get."

"Oh, I don't think so." She looked at him, examined the firm set to his jaw, the tightness of his lips. He didn't like talking about himself much, did he?

"Come on," she prompted. "You like this place more than you'll admit. You came back here. You've gotten yourself involved in this part of the operation… Why do you fight it so hard?"

He turned his head and met her gaze, though he kept his emotions shuttered away so she couldn't really read his face. "I never said I hated this place. I probably love it the most out of the three of us. So don't you question that, Kailey."

"Then why are you so determined to leave?"

His lips thinned further. "Just because I care about the ranch doesn't mean I want to come back. Doesn't mean I belong here. So get that out of your head, okay? I get enough of that from Lacey and Duke. I don't need it from you, too."

"Sheesh. Sorry." He was so touchy about it. "Did something happen to drive you away? I'm just trying to understand, Ry. Things just don't add up."

"Well, that's life," he replied bitterly. "And for the record, I wasn't driven away. I was taken away. Big difference."

She would have asked more, but the screen door slammed up at the house and both of them turned to see Quinn and Duke coming down the driveway to the barn. Just the men. Carrie and Lacey didn't join them.

"Hey, Kailey," Duke called out as they approached. "Thanks for coming over."

"No problem. Ry and I were just talking about this guy here. What's his name, Ry?"

"Rattler."

She grinned. "I like it. Strikes fast and a little bit dangerous. Just like you want."

Quinn smiled. "Well, the problem is we can't really take him at his name, you know?"

Duke nodded. "You're a good judge, Kailey. What do you think of Rylan's purchase?"

She looked at Rylan. Saw defiance in his eyes, but something else, too. Hope. He really wanted this to work. And she wanted it, too. For Crooked Valley. And, on a more unsettling note, for him.

"Well, at face and name value, he's great. I was just telling Rylan that if you bred him with Candyfloss, you'd have a horse like a tank. But the bigger question is bucking ability. I'd like to have a look at his papers. Ry says he competed for a while until he became too valuable as a stud. That natural bucking ability is important. I'd like to see someone get on him. Try to stay on."

Ry's eyes lit up. "It'd give us a chance to see him in the chute, too."

Duke looked his brother in the eye. "You're dying to get on him, aren't you?"

"He hasn't competed in a few years. But yeah. I'd like to see what he's made of. That instinct doesn't just go away."

"Let's do it," Quinn said.

Kailey was usually right in the mix back at her own place, but tonight she stood back and watched, just for this once. She wanted to get a good look at how Rattler handled, his temperament, how he was in the chute. She and Duke went to the small arena and stood at the rails as Quinn and Rylan prepared horse and rider for the main attraction.

"You really think this horse was worth the money?" Duke asked. "Because it's a hell of an impulse buy. Rylan can be so reckless."

It scared her how quickly she wanted to leap to Ry's defense. "Time will tell, Duke. But he didn't buy some old nag, I can tell you that. If I were in the market I would have given him a second look. And I can guarantee you he would have gone for more at auction. If this ride is anything at all, your brother just brought home a bargain."

Duke's jaw dropped a little. "You think so?"

"You need to have more faith in your

brother, Duke. He's a pro rider. He knows what he's doing. And it wasn't nearly as impulsive as you might think."

"What do you mean?"

She watched as Quinn and Ry got Rattler in the chute, as Ry perched up on the rails, waiting for the right moment to ease his weight into the saddle. "I mean Rylan asked me about the program here not long after he first arrived. I agreed with him that the place needed a boost to your breeding program, but we both knew money was an issue. He's trying to help, Duke. And he's the one bearing the financial risk. Don't be too hard on him."

She held her breath as Rylan positioned himself on Rattler's back, and then gave Quinn a sharp nod to open the chute.

Rattler burst forth with strength and aggression, bucking with a power that surprised and delighted Kailey. A grin spread over her face and her eyes were glued to the spectacle as she said to Duke, "Retired my patootie. Look at him go!"

And it wasn't just Rattler. Rylan spurred him on, gorgeous form as he gripped the rope with one hand and held the other aloft. He was a beautiful rider, and while the two were at cross purposes—one trying to rid himself of his cargo and the other trying to stay on—it was almost as if they were working as a team to provide the best ride possible.

Rattler gave a quick and sudden lurch to the side and she saw Ry slip a little, but then he purposefully dismounted, landing on the soft loam of the arena. He got up and brushed off his jeans, a huge smile on his face as Rattler continued around the circle, smaller, quick bucks punctuating his gait.

"Did you see that?" Rylan called out. "Whooeee!"

"He didn't get rid of you," Duke pointed out.

Rylan swaggered over, his hat in his hand. "That has more to do with the quality of the rider than the horse, bro."

Duke rolled his eyes while Kailey chuckled. "Nothing wrong with your ego," Duke muttered.

Ry's face still glowed with excitement, but he became more serious as he met Kailey's gaze and then Duke's. "Let's be honest. A less experienced rider wouldn't have stood a chance. And he's been out of competition for a few years now."

Duke nodded. "And you think he'll earn his keep?"

Kailey looked at Rylan, not Duke, when she cut in. "Brandt can get the ball rolling on that score," she said.

Rylan's gaze was warm. "Thank you, Kailey."

"Don't thank me. This is business, remember?"

But she knew he was thinking—as she was—about that night at the creek, when he'd first asked for her help.

Rylan looked at Duke and held out his hand. "We have a deal then? Ownership stays with me and Crooked Valley reaps the proceeds."

It was a hell of a gift. Kailey hoped Duke realized how much.

"We have a deal," Duke replied, taking his brother's hand.

Rylan stayed true to his word. While ownership of Rattler was in his name, as far as he was concerned, nothing had changed. He'd given his ideas to Quinn, and then he'd hooked up the camper and the highway had become his home.

June became July. July morphed into August, hot and dry, and he was getting tired of the travel and the fair ground and diner food. What he was really craving was a batch of Lacey's fried chicken and a slice of her apple pie. He collected prize money and stayed at the top of the rankings, but at night, when everything was quiet and he was in his camper alone, it was Kailey he thought of most. Kailey swimming in her underwear, challenging him. Kailey in that pretty blue dress from the wedding, smelling like flowers and tasting like summer.

It was better he stay on the road. And away from her. When he was with her, he forgot a lot of things. Like why he didn't want to settle down in the first place. If anything, his feelings for her drove the point home.

He flipped over on the hard mattress and punched his pillow.

He had too much damned time to think, that's what. And he could blame it all on Duke and Lacey and their stupid summons. He was such an idiot. He'd liked the idea of being needed for once in his life, and the chance to prove to his brother and sister that he wasn't just a screwup who'd hit the highway as soon as he'd been old enough. He'd always been the youngest, the tagger-on, the one people felt they had to take care of but never bothered asking what he wanted.

He flipped again. Wondered where all the control he'd managed to attain over his life had fled.

Control.

He sighed, giving up on sleep and staring at the ceiling. That was what this came down to, wasn't it? A need to control his life. He absolutely hated being at the mercy of anyone else.

And now that control wasn't working so well. Because he'd made it a policy never to get too close to anything or anyone who could hurt him. And he'd done both in his return to Crooked Valley by caring for both Kailey and the ranch.

And damn, he was lonely.

Before he could change his mind, he picked up his cell and dialed. It took three rings, and then Kailey picked up. "This had better be good, Duggan."

He hadn't thought about caller ID. Or the time. It was after midnight.

"I'm sorry. Go back to sleep."

She sighed. "I haven't been to sleep yet. Though I was almost there."

"Me, too."

"How's things?"

He wondered how to answer. "Good," he said. "Real good."

"Some of our stock was in Cody last weekend. Heard you put on quite a performance."

"It was okay." Truth was, it had been a hell of a weekend with some very tight competition. And he'd come out of it with a sore shoulder and a bruised rib.

"So why are you calling me in the middle of the night, Ry?"

Her voice was soft, the way lovers spoke late at night, in the dark. What was he doing? He should be staying far away. He didn't need to get wrapped up in her, too.

Too? He pinched the bridge of his nose. It wasn't just Kailey; it was the ranch. It was all of it.

"I needed to hear a familiar voice," he replied. "Look, I really am sorry I called so late. I didn't realize the time. I'll let you go."

There was a long pause while neither of them hung up.

"The thing is," she said quietly, "I can't stop thinking about that night of the wedding."

He couldn't either. Or the sight of her in a wet, white bra and panties. But having her admit it took his libido and kicked it into overdrive. Why did she get to him so easily?

"Kailey—"

"That is why you called, right? Because of this thing we have going on that we keep trying to ignore?"

She was so forthright. It was one of the things he really liked about her. She didn't play games. Didn't beat around the bush. She just said what she meant. Even when it wasn't what he wanted to hear. Or when it was what he wanted more than anything. Or both.

"I don't want to think about you as much as I do." He held the phone close to his mouth, as if it made his lips closer to hers.

She laughed, a sexy little ripple in his ear. "Ditto. The big question is why? Why is thinking about me so bad?"

How did he answer that?

"Come on, Rylan. You think I don't see, but I do. You have this face you show to the world but underneath there's a whole lot of complicated stuff going on. You don't want to be at Crooked Valley. You don't want to

be tied down to anyone or anything. Does that seem normal to you?"

He was so surprised by her insight that he couldn't answer. But there wasn't time anyway as she forged on. "Why does the idea of belonging somewhere scare you so much?"

"It's easy for you," he blurted out, wishing he didn't feel so defensive. "You've been in the same place your whole life with the same people. You've always belonged somewhere."

"And you haven't?"

"I did once."

There was silence down the line. And then Kailey asked the simple question with the difficult answer.

"What happened, Ry?"

"It doesn't matter."

"Of course it does. Talk to me, Rylan. Trust me."

Couldn't she see that was part of the problem? He didn't trust people. "I think I've made a habit of only trusting myself, K."

"And you shut other people out."

"I don't get hurt that way."

"Except you're hurting yourself. And you're missing out on what could be important relationships. I don't just mean romance either, Rylan. But with your sister, your brother. Your mom. People who care about you."

His temper flared. "Oh, you mean people who end up leaving?" He sighed. "God, I did not want to get into this tonight. I just wanted to…to…"

"Make a connection," she whispered. "You don't have the corner on feeling alone, you know."

Her? Alone? She was adored by all, the life of the party. How was she alone?

"Kailey, my dad was killed in action. One day he was alive, the next I was told I would never see my father again. It was hard to wrap my head around that concept, because I was used to him being gone on deployment. But it was different, knowing he'd never walk up the driveway again or throw a ball in the yard or take us riding. He wouldn't laugh or smile or kiss my mom, even in front of us. He was just…gone. It was so final."

"I know, Rylan."

"I had the ranch, though. And Joe and Eileen and all the things I loved, until that was taken away, too. My mom never asked what I wanted. She just decided that we were leaving and moving to Helena. I hated it there. I was a square peg in a round hole. Once I even tried to run away and go back to the ranch."

"How old were you?" she asked, her voice gentle.

"Seven."

"Oh, Rylan."

"Everything was completely out of control. Lacey didn't miss the ranch like I did, and Duke was far more interested in being like our dad to worry about me and what I wanted. So, I got through it. I was the afterthought tagged on the end of the family. And when I was old enough, I did what I wanted. What I'd always wanted."

Wow. He took a deep inhale. He'd never told anyone all that before. Maybe it was because it was Kailey. Maybe because they were on the phone and not face-to-face, and the bit of distance helped.

"So, why didn't you just go back to the ranch?"

Why hadn't he? He'd asked himself that question several times, and all he could come up with was because it was a reminder of his worst memories. "Because it hurt too much. I just wanted to forget the past, leave it behind me and make a new future. But thanks to Joe I got dragged back home anyway."

He could hear her breathing. It was so still. Finally, gently, she spoke.

"Do you realize that you just called Crooked Valley home?"

He hadn't.

"Rylan, I understand that you're hurt. You were so young to lose a parent and to be uprooted. Then to feel like you didn't fit in… I understand, too, that you made a choice to live your life on your terms. There is nothing wrong with that. Just…think about why you're doing things. Is it because it's what you want or because you're trying to protect yourself?"

"No one gets to call the shots in my life again." His voice was firm.

"But you're not calling the shots either," she reminded him. "Fear is. That doesn't sound like a fun way to live."

"It was until the past two or three months."

"Like having a one-night stand in a budget motel?"

Embarrassment flooded through him. "I thought we weren't going to mention that again."

"I wasn't. Except I'm starting to realize that your life on your terms probably isn't making you all that happy."

This was not how he'd wanted this conversation to go. "Listen, I didn't call to get in to all this. I was just by myself and thought…"

Lonely, he reminded himself. Dammit.

"Rylan, I stopped hating you for that night a while back. I had to get over my pride and feeling humiliated. That's all. But I think since then we've started to become friends, you know? I'm only saying these things as a friend who cares. You can't live your life in a bubble without letting anyone in."

Friends. Not that he'd say it, but he had a hard time thinking of Kailey as just a friend. Perhaps it would work better if he could stop wanting more. But she'd put an end to that. She also wasn't the only one with some pride, and he resented the way she made it sound as if she had it all together.

"Really, Kailey? Because I think you do a pretty good job of living in a bubble, too. The only difference is you hide behind your ranch. Hell, you still live with your parents. Talk about putting the kibosh on anyone getting too close. How about lack of privacy as a convenient excuse?"

Silence.

He hadn't meant to lash out. It was just… he hated that she was right, even a little bit. And, he admitted to himself, he was a little bit frustrated. Because Kailey seemed perfectly able to think about them as friends when he couldn't. Couldn't think of her in a solely platonic way. Couldn't get her off his mind. Couldn't go through a whole day without thinking about kissing her again. Seeing her smile.

His head was starting to ache now.

"I'm sorry," he murmured.

"No, I deserved that," she said back. "If I'm going to judge and give free advice, I should expect the same in return."

He'd say this for her. She was fair.

"I've never met anyone like you, K."

"Of course you haven't."

He laughed in spite of himself, resting his hand on his forehead, half out of frustration and half from amusement.

"Hey," she said softly. "I wasn't trying to pick a fight. It's just that the more we…I mean, the more I see you, the more I realize that you're not exactly the person you show to the world. Maybe it's time for you to stop running, Rylan. The way I need to stop settling."

He swallowed hard. He knew he put distance between himself and people he cared about. It was a self-preservation mechanism he'd perfected long ago. It wasn't something he could just stop doing. But what did she mean, settling? Did she mean settling for him? Because she was right on that score. A woman like Kailey deserved better than a rodeo drifter with no fixed address, a camper and one horse to his name.

"Listen, I really do have to go," she whispered. "You gonna be okay?"

"Sure. I'll be home next week anyway. Heading down to Oklahoma before taking a bit of a break."

"Drive carefully."

"I always do."

"And good luck."

"Thanks."

There was an awkward silence for a few beats. "Kailey, thanks for the talk. I don't think I've ever told anyone that before, you know?"

"You're welcome, Ry. Be safe."

In his head he knew the words could be a simple goodbye, but as he clicked off the phone it felt like they were something different. An endearment, two words that meant someone out there was waiting for his return, cared if he made it back in one piece.

Chapter 7

Crooked Valley Ranch was a beehive of activity. As the end of July approached, so did Carrie's due date. When she went into labor ten days early, no one was entirely prepared. Duke disappeared to the hospital. Quinn manned the ranch, while Lacey cooked and cleaned and baked and kept everyone updated as Duke texted her with their progress.

Kailey had been too busy working to spend much time with the Crooked Valley crew, but this morning she came over, both to bring a baby blanket that her mother had knitted and also to put a proposition to Quinn.

She dropped off the blanket to Lacey in the big house, taking a moment to inquire about Carrie and long enough to accept a fresh doughnut still warm from the grease. Quinn came in for a cup of coffee, and Kailey took the opportunity to speak to him about his house, which was newly renovated and sitting vacant now that he and Amber were living at Crooked Valley. She was just walking across the yard with a second doughnut in her hand when she heard an engine and saw a puff of dust. Rylan's truck came into view and her heart gave a little thump.

She'd thought about him often since his late-night phone call. And she kept picturing a cute little boy who'd lost his dad and who had been forced to move away from the only life he'd ever really known. Rylan always seemed so confident, even cocky. But it was all an act. Deep down, he was afraid of being hurt. Of letting himself care for anyone who might let him down.

He'd been right about her, too. She'd focused on work for so long that she'd forgotten that she had a life outside the ranch that she needed to live. She wondered what he'd say about the latest development.

He stopped. She saw the driver's side door open and a pair of dusty boots hit the gravel.

She couldn't help it. A smile broke out on her face. She was glad to see him. Besides, he probably didn't know about Carrie if he'd been driving all morning, and…

He came around the hood of his truck and she halted in her tracks.

A navy sling cradled his right arm close to his body. His gait had a hitch to it, and when her gaze darted to his face she saw scrapes running down one cheek and a dark bruise around his right eye and eyebrow.

All the things she'd said about keeping her distance faded, and she rushed to greet him, concern sending chills down her body. "Oh, my God! What happened to you?"

He smiled, and she noticed his lip had a split that kept him from opening his mouth wider. "Nothing too serious. Minor motor vehicle accident."

"Minor? Look at you!" Gingerly she put her arms around him and held him close. "From the looks of it, you might have been killed. You're okay, right?"

"Easy," he cautioned, his voice gruff. "I hurt all over, Kailey, and I've been sitting in that truck for the past four hours."

His truck. Frowning, she cast a quick look behind him. The truck appeared unscathed.

"Your truck is okay. Did you get it fixed already?"

He shook his head. "Not my truck. I was a passenger, catching a ride back from the bar on Saturday night."

A passenger. Kailey tried to ignore the sharp stab of jealousy and disappointment that rushed through her. She had no claim on him whatsoever. If he'd hooked up with someone after the competition, who was she to judge? After all, wasn't that basically what the two of them had done?

But still. It stung, and the fact that it did made her mad at herself.

"Kailey," he said gently, and she met his gaze. What there was of it, anyway. His left eye was swollen enough that it was half-shut. "I was in a cab. I don't drive after I've had a few."

There was relief, and a little guilt at assuming the worst, but mostly just concern for his injuries. "Are you okay?" she asked again.

He shrugged with one shoulder only. "Not really." His lips formed a bitter line. "I'll heal. But this pretty much ends my season."

His run for the NFR. Kailey's shoulders slumped as she felt the depth of his disappointment. He'd worked hard and she knew he'd coveted a title since he'd started riding broncs. "I'm so sorry," she said. "I know how much you wanted it this year."

"Not your fault." Frustration underlined his voice. "You know, I always thought that if I got injured it would be in competition. Not in a cab on the way back to my stupid camper. Stupid kids out joyriding and hit us broadside. A little bit of fun with a whole lot of consequences."

Before she could say anything, he bit out, "I'm aware of the irony. Ry Duggan, likes a good time, sounding like an old fogy."

"You're angry and frustrated and disappointed. I'd say you're entitled to a little bit of a rant." She peered up into his bruised face. "Truly, though, Ry. The most important thing is that you're okay. What's wrong with your shoulder and is anything else hurt?"

"My shoulder was dislocated. It's back in now but it hurts like the devil, and I'm going to have to do physical therapy, of all things. The doctors weren't sure if I'd need surgery or not. I got a good knock to the head, which gave me this lovely shiner, and the glass from the window left a calling card on my face. And I'm bruised. Down my ribs, which miraculously weren't broken. And down my hip and thigh. I swear the whole right side of my body hurts."

"You need an Epsom salts bath," she decreed. "I'm surprised they let you out of the hospital so soon." It was only Monday.

"They didn't have much of a choice." Again he sent her a slightly crooked grin, and she knew he'd probably checked himself out of the hospital. "Look, do you think you could help me set up the camper?"

"Camper?" She stood back. "You know Lacey isn't going to let you do that. You should be in the house, in a decent bed. This is not a time to be stubborn, Rylan Duggan."

"I'm not up to her fussing and fluttering around, okay? I just want my own space." He seemed to weave on his feet a little and alarm rushed through Kailey at the sight of his suddenly pale face.

"You dumb ass," she chided, going to his left side. "You shouldn't even have been driving today. Here, get back in your truck on the passenger side. I have a plan, but it means we have to scoot out of here before

Lacey realizes you've arrived. I can buy you a couple of days of peace and quiet."

"What the heck…?"

"Get in. I'll explain on the way. Unless you want your sister out here."

He obeyed, getting gingerly in the truck as she hopped into the driver's side. In seconds they were headed back down the driveway toward the main road, and less than ten minutes later she pulled into the driveway of a cozy bungalow surrounded by a stand of pines.

"What is this place?"

She reached into her pocket and withdrew a key. "My new home as of this morning. Partially furnished, rent is good." She grinned. "It's Quinn's house. He's been trying to decide what to do with it, and I offered to rent it on a month-to-month basis in the meantime."

Rylan turned slowly to face her. "Kailey, if this is about what I said on the phone the other night…"

"I've been thinking about it for a while, anyway," she admitted. "What you said just gave me the nudge I needed. It's time I got my own place."

She got out of the truck and was around

to his side before his feet had even hit the ground. Oh, he was moving slowly. Not like Rylan at all, who she suspected would power through most injuries without letting on he was hurt.

"Come on. Let's get you settled inside. I'll make a run back to my house to pick up some necessities, but you can at least take a load off."

He walked slowly behind her as she went ahead and opened the door, then walked through the house and opened windows, letting the fresh summer breeze inside. She'd always liked Quinn's house. When Marie had been alive, she'd put her stamp on the décor. But the fire earlier this year had meant renovating, and as a result the main areas of the house were freshly painted and devoid of any personal touch. Kailey didn't feel as if she was walking into someone else's home. She felt as if she was walking into a new possibility. It was quite exciting and long overdue.

The insurance had paid to replace the furniture, so a brand-new sofa sat in the living room. Rylan sank into it, his breath hitching as his muscles protested, and Kailey knelt down before him, helping him take off his boots. She knew what it was like to bruise ribs or anything in the core area. Simple things such as getting out of a chair or bending to take off boots were painful. Muscles a person took for granted suddenly made themselves known. She slipped the boots off his feet and put them beside the sofa. "Lie down. I bet you didn't sleep much last night."

"Not a lot," he admitted. "This is a nice place."

"It's time I did it. I kept telling myself it was money I didn't need to spend, but we're doing well enough now that I think I deserve it."

"Of course you do."

"You're okay here for a while?"

"Peace and quiet. Why wouldn't I be?"

She paused. She'd already told her parents about her idea of renting Quinn's house. She'd gotten the feeling they were almost relieved, though they'd never say so. But she wasn't sure how they'd feel about Rylan staying, even for just a few days as he recuperated. She'd just pick up what she needed to make him comfortable. There was no rush to move all her things in, too. Besides, in a day or two Rylan would be back at Crooked

Valley, sleeping in his camper again. Once the soreness eased he'd feel more like himself.

"I'll be back in a while. The power's still on, but there's no phone hooked up, so if you need anything you'll have to reach me on your cell."

He stared up at her with glassy eyes. "Be careful with my truck."

Right. She'd nearly forgotten they'd brought his rig over. "I'll unhook the camper. Don't worry about a thing."

As she left he eased himself down on the cushions. The long drive really must have sapped all of his energy. She unhooked the camper and leveled it before heading back to her parents' house. She packed toiletries and a few cleaning supplies, a handful of new towels they'd kept on hand for the barn but had never used. She didn't want to take her mom's groceries, so she decided a quick trip into town was in order. By the time she got back to the house it had been two hours, and Rylan was still asleep.

She put the bags down quietly and stared into his face. One other time she'd been awake and watched him sleep. It was no less personal now. After everything he'd said during their late-night phone call, she knew he had to hate being sidelined, being at the mercy of his injuries and forced to stay at Crooked Valley. He looked so vulnerable, so young. Sometimes she forgot that he was the youngest of the Duggans, not even thirty.

Deep down he had an old soul.

Gently, she smoothed a lock of reddish-brown hair away from his brow. He must have been sleeping lightly, because he opened his eyes, his right one still squinted but the left iris was a deep, intense blue.

She slid her fingers away. "Hello, sleepy-head."

"Hey." He moved to sit up and grunted as the muscles protested. "You're back already?"

"I've been gone over two hours."

Rylan moved to stand up, but she heard the gasp of pain as he levered himself off the sofa. "I swear, I get stiffer by the hour."

"I brought salts. I'll run you a bath and fix you something to eat."

"Don't you have work to do? I don't need a baby-sitter."

She shrugged, knowing she could always find work to do. Knowing she often did just to avoid other stuff. "I think the ranch can survive without me for one day. Besides, I needed to pick up some groceries and cleaning supplies."

"Kailey—"

"Shut up, Rylan, and let someone help you for once. You don't have to be so fiercely independent all the damned time."

She left him muttering in the living room, and went to the bathroom to run water in the tub. She added a good dose of Epsom salts to ease his muscles, and got out one of the new towels for when he was finished. As the tub filled, he went to the camper and found clean clothes. It was all good until it was time for him to get undressed.

He got the sling off okay, if somewhat awkwardly, using his left hand. The problem came with taking off his shirt. He couldn't use his right hand to pull the cuff off his left arm or shrug the fabric off his shoulders as he normally would. After watching him struggle and hearing a few choice curse words, Kailey stepped in. She pulled his left sleeve off his arm and then moved to his right side, easing the freed fabric over and off his shoulder and down to his wrist.

"Better?" she asked, her throat tight. With his shirt off she could see the tight curves of his muscles as well as the shocking amount of bruising down his right side. How he must be hurting right now. The desire to lean in and kiss the purple spots was strong, but she held back. Friends only. That's what she'd said. That was what was best for both of them.

"Thanks," he murmured. "I think I can get the rest."

"Call if you need anything. Towel's hanging on the towel bar."

She escaped before he started unbuttoning his jeans, half hoping he wouldn't need help, half hoping he would. But all she heard on the other side of the door were a few scuffling noises and then the soft sound of him sinking into the water of the bath.

She'd been holding her breath and hadn't even realized it.

While he was soaking, she emptied out his duffels and sorted the laundry into piles. The first load was in the washing machine when she went to the kitchen and began unpacking the groceries and supplies she'd bought.

It had been fun and a little bit exciting, knowing that the purchases were for her own place. She literally had nothing, but with what Quinn had left behind, she could make do. It was midafternoon but neither of them had eaten lunch. When the fridge and cupboards were filled with groceries, she started cooking what she'd picked up for a simple but hearty meal: pork chops and baked potatoes and a salad kit.

The chops were sizzling when she heard the squeaky sound of Ry's feet on the bottom of the tub as he got out. She took out butter and sour cream for the potatoes and listened with one ear in case he got into trouble. Minutes ticked by until she heard the bathroom door open.

"Did you manage okay?" she asked, turning around, and then every other thought fell clean out of her head.

He looked good, so good. His hair was wet and tousled around the tanned skin of his face, and he had on a light cotton shirt and clean jeans. The only problem was he hadn't buttoned either, and he held his right arm close to his chest while the sling dangled from his left hand.

"I had help this morning," he confessed. "One of the nurses at the hospital."

"I just bet you did." She teased him, hoping it would dispel the feeling she got in the pit of her stomach just from looking at him.

He grinned. "Apparently some women actually can resist me, you know."

Right. Maybe not everyone looked at Rylan Duggan and got flushed all over. Which meant it might just be her who was crazy.

"It's been almost twelve hours since my last pain pill," he said quietly. "I could use a hand. If you don't mind, that is."

"Of course. Just a sec."

She turned down the chops and met him in the living room. He'd put his sling on the back of the sofa and had sucked in his stomach, trying to manage the button on his jeans with one hand. Heart in her throat, determined to not make a big deal of it, Kailey silently went to him and reached for the waistband of his pants.

His sharp intake of breath pulled his stomach in, but not enough. The backs of her knuckles still touched the soft, warm skin of his belly as she put the rivet through the buttonhole.

"I can zip," he said, his voice strangely husky.

He pulled the zipper to the top and then

Kailey went to work on his shirt buttons. One by one she fastened the buttons, staring at his chest rather than into his eyes. But it didn't matter. The swirl of intimacy still surrounded them. She studied the hollow of his throat, the ruddy color of the little bit of chest hair that curled at the center of his collarbone, the way his Adam's apple bobbed when he swallowed. As she got to the second-last button, she realized that her fingers had slowed, taking their time in covering the distance from waist to neck.

"There," she murmured, her voice cracking a little.

"Can you help with the sling?"

"Of course."

What on earth was wrong with her? She cleared her throat and reached for the sturdy brace, helping him position it just right and making sure it was fastened securely. She stood back. "Nearly good as new," she stated.

"Something smells good," he said, looking over her shoulder. "Are you cooking?"

"We missed lunch. I made an early dinner. It won't be much longer, I don't think."

"I don't know how to thank you."

"Don't thank me yet. I can't cook like

your sister. Besides, you're going to be on your own after dinner. I've got a lot to do."

She headed for the kitchen and he followed her. "I know you do. I really appreciate you giving me a place to stay. You're right. The camper isn't the most comfortable, not now, anyway. And Lacey would hover. Not to mention Duke riding my ass."

Kailey slapped her palm against her forehead. "Oh, my gosh! How could I have forgotten? You haven't heard the news."

Rylan frowned. "What news?"

"Carrie was in labor this morning. Duke texted while I was grocery shopping. They have a bouncing baby boy. A few weeks early and a little under seven pounds. You're officially an uncle."

She was surprised by the look of pleasure that transformed his face. "I already consider myself an uncle to Amber," he confessed. "But Duke has got to be over the moon. Hard to imagine my big brother a father."

"I've only had the one text, but he sounded pleased as punch. Lacey probably knows more if you want to call."

He reached into his back pocket. "That reminds me. I thought I heard my phone buzz while I was in the tub. Maybe it was her." He checked the call log with a few swipes of his thumb. "Yep. One missed call, and it was the ranch. I'll call back in a bit, get more details."

"Do you like kids, Ry?" He was really good to Amber and seemed pleased about the new baby. It would be a surprise, though. Rylan didn't seem the type. He was too much of a free spirit.

"I do, actually," he said. "Kids have generally got it right. They're not old enough to complicate stuff with personal agendas."

Lacey thought about that for a moment. "But, Ry, kids aren't really old enough to understand that life comes with consequences." She turned the burner back up, checked on the potatoes.

She was just reaching for the bag of salad when he spoke again. "I don't think kids are oblivious to consequences," he said, sitting down at the little table and chairs in the eating area. "I think...well, I think they aren't afraid of them yet. Until we make them that way."

It was an interesting thought. She considered the idea for a moment. She agreed children had a wonderful sense of innocence and simplicity. It wasn't until they got older that they understood fear. That they made decisions based on being afraid rather than taking chances and doing the impossible.

But then there were children such as Amber. Such as Rylan.

"You might be right," she agreed and poured lettuce into a bowl. "But you learned fear early on. When your dad died. When you had to move. And Amber has, too. She lost her mother when she was just a toddler. You know things like that shape who we become. You said so yourself."

She looked up, drawn to his gaze. Maybe he'd think her silly but one of the first things she'd noticed way back last Christmas had been his eyes, thickly lashed, a stunning, clear blue. Her mom would call them Paul Newman eyes. Kailey had seen enough of the older movies to agree.

"That's true," he admitted. "But answer me this. If you took a survey of six-year-olds and asked them what they wanted to be when they grew up, and then asked a room full of thirtysomethings, how would the answer differ?"

That made her stop and think. She vaguely remembered being six. But she remembered friends and classmates talking about being movie stars or sports figures or astronauts. There were no limits. Most thirtysomethings she knew were thinking about kids and bills and making the mortgage payments.

"Is that why you don't settle down, Ry? You're avoiding those responsibilities and consequences for as long as possible?"

He lifted one shoulder. "Maybe. There's a TV show I like and one of the guys has this saying: *I reject your reality and substitute my own.* I like to think I've been making my own reality. Calling my own shots." He frowned. "Up until this point, at least. Now I can't ignore consequences and complications. I've wanted that title for as long as I can remember, Kailey. I gotta be honest and say it hurts knowing I'm not going to get it."

"Maybe next year," she suggested. "You'll heal. Be good as new."

"Maybe," he agreed, but his heart didn't sound in it. "For right now I could use one of those pain pills."

She retrieved the bottle, noticed that they were just over-the-counter strength. "No prescription?"

"I don't like taking that stuff. Makes me

dopey. Give me two of those, though. It should take the edge off."

She shook a couple into her hand, gave them to him along with a glass of water. "Dinner shouldn't be long."

"Thanks. I appreciate it."

"I started a load of laundry for you, too. Figured you've been gone a while and could use some clean clothes."

"You don't have to look after me, Kailey. I'll be fine. Really." He popped the pills into his mouth and chased them with a big swallow of water.

"It's nothing I wouldn't do for any other neighbor," she protested. "Seriously."

But the intensity of his gaze said something different. They both knew he wasn't just another neighbor. If he had been, her fingers wouldn't have hesitated over his buttons. She wouldn't still be thinking about kissing him, or about his long legs folded into the steaming bathwater, or wondering how he was going to manage later tonight.

As she served the meal, she told herself she couldn't let it be her problem.

Chapter 8

Rylan tried to roll over and nearly cried out from the pain.

The bed was comfortable enough, or would have been if he didn't ache all over.

The night after the accident, the hospital had kept him doped up on some primo narcotics. Tonight, the acetaminophen wasn't cutting it. He couldn't get comfortable. Moving positions meant engaging core muscles and shifting ribs. He tried lying on his left side but even then, his right hip pained as gravity pulled it down toward the mattress.

He managed to doze off and on, but by the time the sun came up he was sore, exhausted and honestly felt as though he'd been hit by a truck.

Which, of course, he had.

There was no sense in staying in bed. He got up, tried a warm shower to loosen his muscles, searched for coffee and found none. Kailey had called her dad for a ride back to the ranch after dinner so she could get her own truck. Technically, it was her place, but she'd lent it to Rylan rather than staying here herself. She was still determined to keep space between them. Not that he'd be any threat to her anyway.

He checked his watch. Lacey would be up by now, getting breakfast for Quinn, doing all those housewifely things she did nowadays in addition to her accounting business. Heck, she'd even put in that vegetable garden. He'd never pictured her as a farm wife, but he supposed it wasn't that far a stretch. She'd always been a nurturer, wanting children and a home.

She'd definitely have something to eat. Besides, he hadn't called her back as he'd told Kailey he would. Yesterday the idea of hiding away to lick his wounds had been perfect. Today, though, he knew he should face his family. At some point he had to stop being a coward and start having difficult conversations.

He popped a few more pills, but wasn't too hopeful they'd help. He felt every bump and pothole on the drive to the ranch, relieved when he finally crawled his way up the driveway.

He didn't expect to see Kailey's truck in the yard.

Gingerly he climbed out of the truck and made his way to the house.

Lacey met him at the door, a dusting of flour on her cheek and an apron covering her front. "Rylan! You're home! Carrie has a boy!"

He grinned at his sister's enthusiasm. "I know. Have you spoken to Kailey?"

"Not this morning. Did you drive all night?"

"Actually...I stayed at Quinn's—I mean Kailey's—last night."

He took off his hat, and then she noticed his bruised eye.

"Oh dear." Her face fell with dismay. "That's not from a bar brawl, is it? Oh, Rylan."

It irritated briefly that his family was so quick to assume the worst about him. In

February, she'd been suspicious of where he'd gotten the money to bid on the saddle at Quinn's benefit. Duke didn't trust his judgment. Of course, he hadn't really given them reason to in recent years.

Yet the one person who really had a reason to distrust him was the one person who truly seemed in his corner.

Kailey.

"I haven't been in a bar fight in..." He did a mental check. "Years." He smiled at her, trying his charm. "I was, however, taking a cab last Saturday night and we got broadsided."

"What? Are you okay?"

He sighed. "Yes, and I'm dying for a cup of coffee. Can I come in and fill you in on what happened?"

"Of course." She stood back and let him in, and he hesitated before deciding to take off his boots. It wouldn't do to wear them in the house, but damn, it hurt taking them on and off.

He sat on the stairs and by the time the boots were off his feet he'd broken into a cold sweat.

When he finally made his way to the kitchen, Lacey's eyes were dark with worry.

She had a fresh cup of coffee waiting for him and was putting a plate in the microwave to reheat. He eased himself into a chair at the table, picked up the cup and took a first, fortifying sip.

Delicious.

"I thought about hiding out at Quinn's for a few days. Kailey told me yesterday that she was going to be renting it, and I wasn't ready to face you and Duke and answer a lot of questions. Or be fussed about."

"What changed?"

He grinned. "No coffee in the house. And realizing that I can't just run away from awkward situations all the time."

She simply waited for him to explain. Which he did, making sure he added the part about Kailey going home last night. "I asked her to keep it a secret. I was kind of licking my wounds, literally and figuratively."

"This means the end of your championship hopes, doesn't it." Her face was sympathetic.

"Yeah, it does." He watched as Lacey went to the microwave and took out the plate she'd put in. When she brought it back the scent of apple pancakes and fried ham hit his nose, and he was glad he'd decided to visit this morning.

She put syrup down beside him and he poured on a generous helping before picking up his fork. "You spoil me," he admitted.

"Maybe it's time you got some spoiling," she observed, taking a seat at the table.

He thought about Kailey last night and her simple but lovely dinner, and how he'd enjoyed talking with her. Normally a scene such as that would have sent him running for the hills. So why wasn't he?

The obvious reason was that he couldn't, not in the shape he was in. But that would be a big fat lie.

"Lacey, when you came back here, you had no intention of staying. What changed your mind? Quinn?"

"Hmm." He chewed and swallowed a mammoth bite of pancake while she considered. "Part of it was Quinn, and part of it was Amber. But there was a time when I was sure we weren't going to work out and I knew I was going to stay in Gibson anyway."

"Why?"

He kept feeding his stomach, hoping to dislodge the weight that seemed to settle right in the pit. He had a feeling he knew what she was going to say.

"I suppose it's because this place has a way of getting into a person's blood. No one could have been more surprised than me, Ry. But there's something about this town, this ranch, that just grounds a person. At first I couldn't imagine staying, and then I couldn't imagine leaving it behind."

Just as he'd thought.

Then again, it was no surprise. He'd had the same feeling when he was five years old. Like this was the best place on earth. And leaving it had left him feeling...

Bereft.

He looked at Lacey and finally grasped what he'd always known in his heart but hadn't been able to quite describe. He'd grieved the loss of his dad. But he'd also grieved the loss of Crooked Valley as much, if not more. It had been perfect. He'd belonged here. He'd felt safe and loved and understood. And then it had been gone.

And by staying away all these years, he'd never had to truly deal with that grief. Until now.

"Ry? Are you okay?"

He swallowed, his throat thick. "Not really. I'm just tired, I guess. I didn't sleep much last night."

"Do you want to stay here?"

He shook his head. "You're newlyweds and a new family. You deserve your honeymoon period."

She grinned and patted his hand. "Well, that's quite a romantic notion, for a rodeo bum."

He smiled back. "I have my moments. Anyway, seriously, a few days at Kailey's and I'll be right as rain and back in my camper."

"Kailey, huh?" Lacey's gaze was sharp.

"It's not like that. Believe me. She made sure to stay at her mom and dad's last night rather than move her stuff in. Kailey's not interested in me that way."

Lacey burst out laughing. "Right. Okay. Whatever." Her tone said that she didn't believe him in the least.

"Hard as it may be to believe, she's pretty determined not to give me another shot. We're just friends." He didn't quite believe that, but there was no other way to describe their relationship when they both felt the pull of attraction and were nothing about it. He raised an eyebrow. "After what happened in February, that in itself is a miracle."

"She must believe in you on some level. She took your side with the Rattler issue."

"Horses are a different matter." Very different from gambling with hearts. "That's business."

Right on cue, the front door slammed and he heard Kailey's voice call out. "Halloo, is the coffee on?"

Lacey grinned and called back, "Of course. And I have cake."

Rylan frowned. "You never said anything about cake."

"You needed a good breakfast."

Kailey stomped into the kitchen in her stocking feet and stopped short when she saw Rylan. "Oh. Hi."

"Hi, yourself. I was filling Lacey in on what happened."

Recovered, Kailey went to the cupboard for a coffee cup. "I came over to get the goss on the new baby." She smiled at Lacey. "When are mama and baby headed home? Maybe I'll make a run in later today to visit."

"Tomorrow, if all goes well. We're going to have a family dinner here, quiet-like. You should come."

Kailey shrugged. "I'm not family."

"The hell you aren't." Lacey sent her a firm look. "I know for a fact you and Carrie are like sisters. She'd be hurt if you weren't here, Kailey."

"I'll try. Things are pretty busy."

"It's showery today and it's calling for rain all day tomorrow. You won't be haying. There's no reason why you shouldn't be here," Rylan added. It would be better if things weren't weird between them, wouldn't it? After all, they'd been much better yesterday once they'd sat down to dinner. Platonic. Polite. And then she'd said "see you later" and left him to his own devices.

The phone rang, and Lacey disappeared to answer it. Rylan looked up at Kailey. "In the end, I figured telling her was probably better than hiding out or having her hear from somewhere else." He sent her a winning smile. "Plus there was no coffee at your house."

"Did she freak out?" Kailey took a sip of her brew and watched him over the rim of her cup.

"Not as much as I expected. But the offer to stay was made right away. Do you mind if I stay at yours for another few nights? She and Quinn are newlyweds. It's awkward. Even staying in the camper is pushing it, because I'm in their hair all the time, you know? But at least there's a little privacy."

"Afraid you might get some of that love stuff on you?" She chuckled, then shook her head. "I don't mind. It's so busy right now that I was thinking I'd just take a few things over each time I go by. I won't be ready to really move in until, well, probably the weekend."

"Thanks. I appreciate it. By then I should be fine to move back into the camper again."

She went to the cookie jar and lifted the lid, searching for a treat. Rewarded, she took out a chocolate chip cookie and started to munch. "I see you managed to get dressed all by yourself this morning," she observed, her eyes glinting with mischief as she chewed the cookie.

"It was not a quick job," he admitted. Indeed, he'd struggled most with the button of his jeans. He'd made a quick movement without thinking, and his shoulder had seized and his eyes had watered from the pain. The shirt, though, that had been easier. Time consuming, but easier.

He wiggled the fingers of his left hand,

gesturing for a cookie, and she retrieved him one from the jar. "So, are you really thinking of heading to the hospital later?" he asked.

"How would it look if I didn't visit my best friend when she had a baby?" Kailey asked. "I didn't go last night because I thought it was too soon. But if she's in another day… I should take her flowers or something."

He shoved the cookie in his mouth, washed it down with a gulp of cooling coffee. "Duke's my only brother. I should probably put in an appearance, too. Want to drive together?"

Lacey's muffled voice coming from the office was the only sound in the relative silence.

"For Pete's sake. I'm staying at the place you're supposed to be renting. We run into each other all the time, and you have a vested interest in my new horse." He looked into her eyes. "There is nothing weird about an uncle and honorary aunt visiting the hospital together. Unless you make it weird, in which case I'm going to start thinking this isn't as platonic as you let on."

Boom! It was a good shot, but it didn't have the oomph he thought it might. Maybe because he wasn't thinking platonically about her at all either.

"Fine. We'll save the gas and drive in together. Happy?"

"Immensely. How about I pick you up at four? That way we don't lose the whole workday."

"You're working? Like that?" She nodded toward his sling.

"I want to stop by the barn. Talk to the guys. Check on Rattler. I've been gone awhile. I need to get caught up."

"I guess that'll be okay then."

"We can visit and then stop for a burger on the way back."

"But this isn't a date," she confirmed.

"A man's gotta eat."

She checked her watch. "I gotta run. I came for the update but really I wanted to drop off the first month's rent to Quinn. I didn't expect him to give me the key yesterday, and I don't want to take advantage."

"You might possibly be the most responsible person I've ever known," he said, grinning. "Wait, scratch that. Duke is. But you're a close second."

"Gee, thanks."

She gave his good shoulder a jostle on her way by. "Catch you later."

"Four o'clock. Sharp."

"Yeah, yeah," she called back, and a few seconds later he heard her go out the door.

Lacey was still on the phone, and Rylan took a few moments to think about what was happening. More than that, he wasn't sure what he wanted to do about it. He'd come back to Crooked Valley with the intent of simply using it as a place to park. His goal always had been a run at the championship. In the absence of that goal what was he supposed to do? Part of him wanted to run away. Not let himself get attached again.

The other part told him to stay and see this through. That he couldn't go on running forever. At some point he had to deal with stuff. At some point he had to…

Grow up.

Deep down he knew what he really wanted, and it scared him to death. But he'd known it from the moment he'd loaded Rattler in the trailer and had headed for home.

Home.

Hell of a thing.

Lacey and Duke had been right after all. He'd sworn up and down that coming back wouldn't mean they could count on him to stay. But that was exactly what he was going to do.

Stay.

Chapter 9

Kailey knew it was just a trip to the hospital, but she didn't want to show up in jeans and a T-shirt. At three she called it quits and left the barn in favor of a shower. Now, wearing a sundress and sandals, she put the last twists on the single French braid and wrapped the elastic around the end. For some reason her hair braided easier when it was damp, and she checked the mirror briefly, satisfied with the neat plait. Her freckles were starting to stand out thanks to days in the sun, and a swish of mascara made her eyes seem bigger and a swipe of lipstick highlighted her lips. She hoped it looked like she was trying—but not trying too hard.

Her mom had made cheese biscuits and had packed a half dozen in a zipped plastic bag in case Carrie was getting nasty hospital food. Kailey wasn't the crochet type, so the blue gift bag in her hand held store-bought clothes. Her favorite was the Onesie that said Handsome Cowboy across the front with the picture of a mustache beneath it. She knew Duke would get a kick out of it. There was also a pair of the tiniest jeans she'd ever seen, paired with a soft red-and-blue plaid shirt.

This little guy was going to be a rancher all the way.

"Rylan's here!" her mother called.

"Thanks, Mom." Kailey made her way toward the front room. She rather hoped to get out before her mom had the opportunity to say anything, but no such luck. Her mother met her in the entry, holding out Kailey's purse.

"Don't forget this. And have fun."

"I'm visiting a hospital, Mom."

"With Rylan Duggan. He's very handsome, you know."

"Yes, I know." She took the purse.

"And you look very pretty, honey."

Kailey smoothed her hand over the skirt of the dress. "Is it too much? I didn't want to look like I'd gone right from the barn or smell up the hospital."

"No, it's not too much. Give Carrie and Duke our love. And take a few pictures with that phone of yours."

"I will." On impulse she leaned over and kissed her mother's cheek before opening the door and stepping out onto the porch.

Rylan had shut off the truck and was walking across the yard, but he stopped when he saw her. A low whistle sounded from his lips. "Shee-oot," he said, grinning at her. "You dressed up and everything."

She scowled. "I do own clothing other than jeans and shirts."

"Yes, you most certainly do, Miss Brandt." He backtracked to the truck and opened the passenger-side door. She hoped she wasn't blushing as she climbed into the cab and he shut the door behind her.

On the seat beside her was a tote bag and a teddy bear with a blue gingham ribbon around its neck. "You went shopping?" she asked as Rylan got in and started the truck by reaching around the steering wheel with his left hand.

"Just a stop at the store in town. Lacey went to visit before lunch and said that Carrie had put in a request for some clothes. I guess they weren't quite ready to leave for the hospital when Carrie went into labor." He chuckled as they started out the driveway. "Duke's only been home long enough to get a few hours sleep and have a shower, and he was so anxious to get back, he forgot to pack what she'd asked for. Lacey says he is one proud papa."

"Of course he is. Especially since this is his first baby."

It seemed Rylan was true to his word about the platonic thing. On the way to the hospital they chatted about Crooked Valley, the changes Rylan wanted to implement in the program, things Kailey had done with Brandt stock and the plausibility of implementing similar practices at the Duggans'. Nothing personal, no innuendos. It was nice, she realized. As Ry sang Rattler's praises, she discovered she'd missed this kind of chat in recent months. She and Carrie had often shared work talks, but since Duke's arrival, her friend had been preoccupied with love and babies. So, too, with Quinn. His focus was on Lacey now and a brand-new family. Not Rylan, though. No romance and babies for him.

Her relief was tempered by a slight thread of disappointment, which was absolutely ridiculous. Romance and babies weren't what she wanted from him. She really didn't want anything, besides peace.

They arrived and made their way to the maternity wing, treading softly as they approached the correct room number. Kailey peeked around the corner of the door and saw Carrie sitting up in bed, flipping the pages of a magazine while a nursery bassinette sat beside the bed.

"Knock knock," she called softly.

Carrie looked up and a smile lit her face. "Hi! Come on in." Her voice was clear but hushed. "He's sleeping right now. Perfect time for visitors."

Kailey stepped in, feeling as if she was in another world. Sure, she'd been around babies now and again. She'd babysat occasionally growing up and she'd always been close to Amber, Quinn's daughter. But her best friend, as a mom…it did something to her. Made her happy and sad and a little bit broody. Had her dedication to Brandt Ranch cost her something important? What might have happened if Colt hadn't withdrawn his proposal?

"You look wonderful," Kailey said, and Rylan trailed into the room behind her. "Mom sent you biscuits and honeyed butter. And Rylan brought you your clothes."

Ry held up the bag. "Lacey packed it. I didn't go through your delicates."

Carrie choked on a laugh. "Oh, God, the very idea of delicates right now is...well, comical."

Rylan blushed. Kailey grinned.

"Where's Duke?"

"On a sandwich run. I'm dying for a turkey sub and a glass of cold milk."

Kailey peered into the bassinette. The junior Duggan was sleeping, his tiny lips sucking in and out, a pale fringe of red hair peeking around a stretchy blue cap. He was swaddled in a flannel blanket, and looked so tiny and fragile that Kailey caught her breath.

"He's beautiful, Carrie. Just beautiful. Ry, come see."

Rylan dutifully peeked at the baby and Kailey watched as his face softened, mellowed. What kind of father would he make? Kind, she figured. Probably patient.

But restless. And whoever married him would have to get used to his itchy feet. He didn't like to stay in one place for long, didn't like to be fenced in, did he? It would be like permanently stabling a bronco who longed to run wild in a pasture thick with rich grass. A punishment.

"Have you named him yet? Lacey never said."

"Evan Joseph." Duke's voice came from the doorway and he stepped inside as they turned to look at him. He was grinning from ear to ear, puffed up as any proud papa would be, carrying a paper sack of sandwiches, a can of soda and a bottle of milk.

"After our father and his father," Rylan said softly.

"Do you mind?" Duke met his brother's gaze, his face losing its joviality and turning serious.

"Of course not." Rylan held out his left hand to Duke. "It's a fine name, Duke. Congratulations."

Kailey watched as Duke put down the food and shook Rylan's hand, their gazes holding. Something was different tonight, something in the way they were with each other. More...equal. It didn't really make sense, as she didn't think anything had really changed. Heck, Rylan had been gone for weeks. When had there been time for them to hash out their differences? Last she'd seen, Duke was still ticked at Rylan for buying Rattler without his input.

"Sorry to hear about your accident," Duke said, nodding at the sling. "Glad you're all right, though. Guess this changes a few things, huh?"

Rylan nodded. "Unfortunately. If it's all right with you, I'll stay through until Christmas. Work with the bucking stock. That way the terms of the will'll be met and Crooked Valley will be in the clear. All yours."

Duke looked at Carrie, who smiled encouragingly, and then back at Rylan. "Wow. I appreciate that, Ry. Big-time."

"I know it's what you want. What Lacey wants. That's why I came back, after all. It's not your fault I can't compete for now."

Kailey tried not to let her mouth drop open. Rylan was staying? For at least another four months? When he'd been traveling while competing it had been easier to deal with the temptation he presented. He was only around now and again. But four months… Sixteen weeks. Hoo-boy.

Carrie spoke up from the bed. "We'll have to decide what to do with your third, Rylan. We can maybe put together enough money to buy you out, if that's what you want."

He nodded. "We can talk about that when the time comes. No need to worry about that now." He looked down at the baby. "Seems to me we have something here a little more important that takes priority."

Duke reached into the bassinette and picked up the baby, holding him by the bottom and cradling his head in his big palm. "You're right," he agreed. Even though the baby was sleeping, Duke spoke to him. "Evan, meet your uncle Ry and your aunt Kailey."

Kailey's face heated. Had Duke paired up their names on purpose?

Duke held out his hands, offering Evan to Kailey first. "Do you want to hold him?"

She did. She blinked, thinking about how she'd had a chance to have a family of her own and had passed it up. Logically she knew there was still a chance. She wasn't exactly old. But it definitely felt as though her options were limited, and seeing her friends marry and have families just drove the point home.

She'd made her choice. It wasn't likely that situation would change, either.

But for now she held out her arms and accepted the small, warm bundle into her embrace. Evan's tiny head rested in the curve of her elbow as she looked down into the angelic face. He'd awakened, not fussing, but with dark, unfocused eyes staring at her.

"Well, hello there," she said softly, feeling her heart turn over. Babies were so innocent, so helpless. So…precious. "You and me, we're gonna have some fun. I'm gonna teach you to climb that old oak tree behind the big house, and we'll catch tadpoles in the pond and get good and dirty. Just you wait."

She looked up at Carrie. "You did good, hon. He's awesome."

"We think so. At least for now. Talk to me in a few days when I haven't had any sleep."

Any jealousy Kailey might have felt was short-lived. Carrie had no family left. She was an only child and her mother had died of cancer a few years earlier, and her father had taken off. It was so good to see Carrie happy and contented. "You are going to be spoiled rotten. Lacey and I are going to see to it that you get some downtime to sleep. We'll be fighting over who gets to babysit."

"I feel very lucky," Carrie replied, patting the bed. Kailey went and sat beside her on the mattress, Evan still snuggled in her arms. "I never expected this. And I don't feel so alone. It's nice to know that you're close by, and Lacey, too. Helen is even coming for a week to help out."

The baby felt very right in Kailey's arms. She leaned back against the pillows and nudged Carrie. "Look at that. I thought Duke was still mad at Rylan."

The brothers were sitting in two vinyl armchairs, chatting away effortlessly.

"I know it sounds terrible, but I'm almost glad that Rylan was in that accident," Carrie said.

"What? But why?" Kailey recalled all the bruising down Rylan's side and cringed. "He's really banged up, you know. Lots of bruising you haven't seen."

"And you have?" Carrie's words were laced with delighted curiosity.

"Not like that. I helped him get his shirt off yesterday, that's all."

"Sounds like enough to me," Carrie responded, grinning.

"You still haven't told me why you're glad this happened?" Kailey frowned, trying to keep the conversation on track. "Ry's incredibly disappointed. He really had a shot, you know?"

Carrie met her gaze. "You really care about him, don't you?"

She hoped she managed to keep her poker face. "I don't hate him anymore, and that's a big step."

"Well, Duke and I think that Rylan's been running from something. Maybe this accident is what will make him stop running and think about settling down."

"I've had the same thought myself. But what would he have to run from?" Kailey shifted the baby a bit, getting more comfortable.

"Duke doesn't know. He just knows that once Rylan turned eighteen he was gone. He's done nothing but move around since. Ranch to ranch, place to place, rodeos every other weekend. Avoiding anything that might be construed as a commitment."

Kailey looked up and found Rylan's gaze on her. Something warm and feminine curled through her insides, having him look at her like that.

She shifted her attention back to Carrie. "Maybe he just wanted a different adventure than Duke. You know, Duke was in the army for a lot of years. He got to move around, see different things, different people. I'm not saying it was easy…not at all. But maybe we're all a little quick to judge."

Carrie nudged her. "Oh, girlfriend, you've got it bad. You're defending him now."

Kailey shook her head. "What he did in February was wrong. I don't defend those actions at all. I'm just saying maybe people shouldn't be so quick to dismiss him."

And maybe that had been the problem all along. He'd said something about always feeling like the tagger-on, either in the way or invisible. Maybe Carrie was right. Maybe staying on at Crooked Valley was just what Rylan needed for his family to take him seriously.

Except she'd distinctly heard him say the words *until Christmas*. Nothing long term or indefinite.

She'd monopolized Evan for long enough, so she got up off the bed and walked over to where Rylan was sitting. "You want to try, Uncle Ry?"

"I've only got one arm," he cautioned. "Maybe I shouldn't."

"Your left one works fine and he's just a little thing. I'll help. You can't visit and not at least hold him for a few minutes."

He curled his arm into position and Kailey slid the baby into the strong curve, making sure his head was supported and he was held nice and tight. Rylan adjusted his shoulder and posture. "Well, would you look at that," he murmured. "Gosh, he's just a little mite. Hardly weighs anything."

"Until he cries," Duke said. "Then he gets real big, real fast."

They all laughed. Rylan settled back in the chair while Duke handed Carrie the milk and unwrapped her sandwich. The talk was much lighter as they visited, and when the food was gone, Kailey went to work and brushed and braided Carrie's hair as a treat.

"Lacey packed real pajamas for you in there," Kailey said, nodding toward the tote bag. "Tomorrow you'll be home and you can have a shower in your own bathroom and sleep in your own bed."

"That sounds heavenly."

By that time Evan was really awake and unhappy, looking for his next meal. When

Carrie blushed, Kailey understood that she was going to nurse and that she wasn't quite comfortable doing that in front of people—in particular her brother-in-law.

"We should probably get going anyway," Kailey suggested. "Rather than outstay our welcome."

"I'm awfully glad you came," Carrie said, and Duke gave Kailey a quick hug. Rylan leaned over and kissed Carrie's forehead in a tender gesture that softened Kailey's heart even further.

"We'll see you in a day or so. Call if you need anything, okay?"

He really had to start being not so nice.

They headed back toward Gibson, making a pit stop along the way for supper. True to his word, Rylan sprang for burgers and fries, and they sat in his truck and ate them with the windows rolled down, Rylan manhandling his sandwich with one hand. It was about as un-date-like as Kailey could imagine, yet there was something rather intimate about sitting there with a surprisingly humid breeze pulling through the cab. The showers that had been forecast hadn't arrived yet, but as Kailey ate her fries she knew rain was coming. There was a smell in the air, a taste that she'd experienced many times over the years.

They didn't talk. There'd been a lot of talking the past few days, and instead they simply sat and ate, and enjoyed the fresh air and greasy food.

Finally, when the last fry had been eaten, and Kailey took a long pull on her soda, Rylan spoke.

"Thunderstorms are rolling in."

Indeed, the sultry air had gone cold, and the wind shushed through the leaves in a telltale whisper of impending bad weather. Through the windshield, Kailey saw dark clouds towering in the sky, gray and menacing. "Damn," she murmured. "I hope everything was dried and baled this afternoon. I probably shouldn't have gone tonight."

"Not much you can do about it now," Rylan said reasonably. They watched through the window as the cloud built and shifted, drawing nearer. A spear of lightning forked toward the ground, and despite the noise from traffic on the highway beside them, they heard the rumble of distant thunder several seconds later.

"Do you want to try to head back now, or sit through it and wait?"

"Let's drive," she said. "Rain's forecast for tomorrow, too. The showers could last for hours."

"You got it."

They were almost to Gibson when the sky darkened and the thunder could be heard over the rumble of the engine. A gust of wind grabbed at the truck, and Rylan's lips formed a grim line. "Damn, I think we're in for it now."

He no sooner got the words out of his mouth than the sky opened up, hammering down huge droplets of rain that sounded like gravel hitting the truck. Rylan turned on the wipers full blast, but the road ahead was a wall of water, reducing visibility to a few feet. He slowed, put on his four-way flashers, and when a dirt range road appeared on the right, he turned off the main drag away from other traffic.

"Wow," Kailey said, frowning. Rain was a welcome sight in summer, but not this kind, not such a downpour that it caused crop damage and run-off and flash floods.

"Wow is right," he replied, pulling off on the wide shoulder. "We might as well ride the worst of it out. You don't have a deck of cards or something in that bag, do you?"

She snorted out a laugh as he cut the engine. Without the purr of the motor, the rain was a rhythmic pounding that sheltered them from the outside world.

"Afraid not. But I have a pad of paper. We could play hangman."

His sideways grin was back. "I know who you'd like to hang," he said acidly. "Me."

"Eh, not so much these days. I'm getting used to you." She raised her eyebrow, arched it at him saucily. "That doesn't mean I·like you, by the way."

"You did offer your house," he reminded her.

"Because I felt sorry for you," she replied.

"Damn," he said softly. "This is why I like you, Kailey. You never give an inch and you make me laugh."

She wanted to say likewise, but he didn't need the encouragement.

The noise on the roof of the truck intensified, and their smiles faded. "Hail," she breathed, knowing it could cause so much damage. Even with their limited vision they could see the white balls of ice bouncing off the windshield and hood.

The first storm cell eased, and Kailey thought for a minute they were going to be able to leave. But then a second cell came right behind it, complete with flashing lightning and cannon-like thunder. The safest place for them right now was exactly where they were.

She looked over at Rylan, who was staring grimly out the driver's side window. "Mind if I ask you something?"

He shrugged. "Would it matter if I did mind?"

"Probably not," she answered honestly. "There's a consensus among your family that you've spent your adult life running from something. Is there any truth in that?"

He snapped his head around to stare at her. "Is that what they're saying?"

She nodded. "That there has to be a reason why you left as soon as you were done high school. Why you haven't settled anywhere. In fact, I think you surprised the hell out of them by coming back at all."

"I like what I do. That's all."

She wondered if he'd open up if she opened up first. "I get the not wanting to be vulnerable, Ry. At the wedding when you asked why I wasn't hitched? I had a real answer that I didn't want to tell you."

"Yeah?"

"Colt Black asked me last fall. We'd been seeing each other for a while. I thought we were crazy about each other. He works in a feedlot up around Cut Bank. When he realized I wouldn't just up and leave the ranch behind, he changed his mind."

"He withdrew his proposal?" Rylan's eyes widened. "Are you serious?"

"Very." She twisted her hands in her lap. She didn't like talking about it, which was why the only person who knew what had happened was her mom. It had been impossible to hide her distress the night he'd broken it off.

"But…cripes, Kailey. You run the ranch. It couldn't run without you."

"That's what I said." She shook her head. "According to Colt, a woman followed her husband, not the other way around. I had no idea he was so…shortsighted."

"Not to mention sexist," Rylan added. "You're better off, trust me."

"I know," she whispered, her voice barely audible above the racket of the storm. "But it still hurts sometimes. I know I come across as Fun Kailey. And up until the past year or so, that was enough. But seeing Carrie so happy and Lacey...I realized I want those things, Rylan. And I almost had them."

He turned in the seat, unbuckling his seat-belt so he could face her better. "Listen," he said firmly. "Having it doesn't matter if it's with the wrong person."

She knew he was right.

Just as she knew he wasn't the right person either.

"I know that. Deep down, I do. Anyway, that's why I'm not hitched. I'm pretty much married to Brandt Ranch, and it comes with the package."

Rylan nodded. "It's a hell of a legacy. Of course you want to stay there."

She was puzzled now. "Okay, so Crooked Valley is *your* legacy. Why fight taking on your third? You always wanted to be a cow-boy. You loved it here as a kid. I know you said it hurt too much to come back, but now you're here. What's keeping you from going all the way?"

He sighed, slumped in his seat. "I don't know. Fear? Stubbornness? I made myself a promise the day we drove away from here and moved to Helena. I promised myself that when I was old enough I would always, al-ways call the shots in my own life. That no one could make me go anywhere I didn't want. I cried every night for months, wanting to come back here. My best friend was a fifteen-year-old pony named Daisy, and everyone treated me like she was a stupid pet who didn't matter and I should just get over it. I had no say. My opinion was brushed off because I was a little kid."

"Are you still angry at your mom?"

His brows pulled together as he thought. "No, not really. The ranch was my dad's family's place, and without him she didn't feel at home. She wasn't a farm girl. And she had a family to support after he was gone. She did what she had to do. I understand that. She made her decisions and I've made mine. The thing is…"

He paused then. Looked at her and then looked away. "Never mind."

For him to stop so suddenly, she knew what he'd been going to say was important.

She reached over and put her hand on his knee. "What is it, Ry?"

His gaze met hers. "I didn't want to come back here because I was afraid I'd turn into that scared little boy again. God, that sounds silly."

"No," she answered, squeezing his thigh.

"No, it doesn't. Our memories shape us into who we become. Sometimes we embrace them. Sometimes we wish we could leave them behind."

"I hate fear, do you know that?" His jaw was clenched. "My dad died and I was so scared that something might happen to my mom and we'd be left alone. Then Duke joined the army and I was afraid he'd be killed. I hate that helpless feeling."

"And yet your passion is doing something that has the potential to hurt you."

He pondered for a moment. "You know, it's my way of giving fear the finger. I will never, ever let myself be so vulnerable that I turn into that frightened little boy again."

Such as staying in one place too long. Such as forging meaningful, long-term relationships. The pieces came together for her now. It was all about self-preservation for Rylan. And damned if she didn't understand it. Wasn't that what she'd been doing for the past year?

"We end up doing some strange things in the name of protecting our hearts," she mused. "Like Valentine's Day. After we broke up, Colt moved on so fast he nearly gave himself whiplash. It stung. But when you showed up at the dance…I guess I thought it would be a good idea to show him what he'd tossed away."

Rylan's jaw dropped. "You mean I was revenge sex?"

Her cheeks heated. "This is where I owe you the apology, Ry. I was so hard on you for running out that morning, but my motives were far from pure where you were concerned. I own part of the blame for what happened."

He put his left hand to his chest. "Oh, my God. You've just shredded the last bit of my pride."

A small smile crept up her cheek. "I'm sorry, okay? I should never have gotten up on my high horse and been so rough on you. It was pride, pure and simple. Humiliation. I wasn't proud of myself, and when I woke up I had to face the music."

"I seriously think my feelings are hurt."

She patted his knee. "If it's any consolation at all, once we hit the sheets Colt Black was the furthest thing from my mind."

She'd meant to make it sound like a joke, but once the words were out there they were really out there.

Rylan let out a soft curse. "You need to

warn a guy before you say something like that, K. Because if you're trying to make me forget that night, that's not the way to do it."

And neither was saying that. The rain still poured, and their minutes spent inside the truck had steamed up the windows. They were in their own little world, on a side road in the middle of a storm and nothing to do but fight the temptation that was getting heavier in the air by the second.

"Why don't you come over here," he suggested softly, locking his gaze with hers. "Come over here and kiss me like you know you want to."

"Rylan…"

"No revenge, no promises, no skipping out in the morning. Just you and me, Kailey. I'm not sure how much longer we can do this dance without something giving."

Chapter 10

Kailey debated for all of two seconds before she tossed caution to the wind. He was right. They'd been fighting this ever since his return. And this time they both knew what they were walking into. And what they weren't.

Desire…it took over and rendered everything else irrelevant. With her gaze locked on his, she unbuckled her seat belt while Ry reached for the lever to push the bench seat all the way back. Her heart pounded and her blood raced as she crawled over the upholstery to straddle him. Everything about him was muscled and hard and sweat pooled at the base of her spine, both from the humid air in the cab and how her body heated just being close to him like this.

She cupped his jaws in her hands and lowered her mouth to his.

His lips were soft, pliant, beguiling. For long moments she simply enjoyed kissing him, tasting him, the textures of his mouth and the way his left arm came around and pressed her closer to him. Her knees were on either side of his hips and without thinking she shifted her pelvis, rubbing against him, until their breath came hard and fast. Need pounded through her, and she found herself thankful that she'd chosen the light sundress over jeans. The cotton skirt pooled around them and the only fabric that stood between her and the denim of his jeans were the silky white panties she wore.

His hand pulled on the sundress strap, sliding it roughly off her shoulder, exposing her breast.

"You didn't wear a bra," he marveled, cupping her in his hand.

"There's one built in," she breathed, and gasped as he replaced his hand with his mouth.

"Rylan," she murmured, overwhelmed. "Ry."

Need took over and she slid a bit backward, fumbling with the button and zip of his jeans, sliding them down and setting him free. Removing her panties proved a little more challenging, but they were both highly motivated now.

Lightning flashed and thunder boomed as she slid back on top of him.

"Be sure," he murmured, putting his palm on her cheek and looking her dead in the eye. "Be really sure, Kailey."

"Shut up, Ry. I don't want to talk. I just want to feel."

He peeled down the other side of her dress and they rode out the storm together.

The windows were thick with steam as the storm eased, both inside and outside of the truck. Kailey reached for the straps of her dress only to find Rylan's gentle fingers there, helping her put her clothing back in place. She retrieved her underwear from the floor and slid it over her legs while Rylan tugged at his jeans with his one good hand.

"Let me help," she murmured, and together they got his pants back on and she had him buttoned and zipped again.

"I think the rain is letting up," he said. He turned the key so that the battery was on and rolled down the window. It was nothing but a light shower now, the violent storm cells moving off to the east.

Kailey moved to her side of the seat and rolled her window down, too, clearing the moisture from the inside of the pane.

The windshield was another story. Rylan turned the key all the way and fired up the defrost. He looked over at her with a lopsided smile. "You okay, Curly?"

The nickname should bother her, but it didn't. "Better than okay," she replied, resting against the back of the seat. "I think I really needed that."

"Me, too."

She chuckled. "Hey, I bet it's been longer for me."

His eyes were so blue that she thought she might drown in them. "Let me guess. February fourteenth?"

She was pretty sure she was blushing. "Uh, yeah."

"Me, too."

That was a surprise. Her head came away

from the back of the seat as she stared at him. "Really? Even with all your travel and the, uh, buckle bunnies?"

"Even with." His gaze softened. "That surprises you?"

"Well, yeah." It gave her a warm, fuzzy feeling, knowing that she'd been the only one since the winter. "You're Rylan Duggan. Sexy bronc rider. Charming drifter."

"Charming, huh?"

"Maybe a little. Mostly a pain in my ass."

The smile he sent her was so sweet her heart ached with it.

"What happens now, Ry? No pressure, okay? I just want to know where we stand. No confusion. No…surprises."

The windshield was starting to clear, and Rylan rolled up his window most of the way to keep the light rain from getting in the cab. "I like you, Kailey. I like you a lot. I like being with you and arguing with you and God knows I like…the sex. I just can't make promises. If you're looking at me like you were looking at this Colt guy—as a settle down forever kind of thing—you're setting yourself up for disappointment. But if you know that going in and you're still interested, I want to see you again. I'm not ready for this to be over."

She'd known before tonight ever happened that this would be the outcome if they ever gave in to their desires. Knowing it didn't stop the little bit of disappointment from hearing him say it, though. If they carried on, it was with the full knowledge that it was short term. An affair.

The big question was how badly did she want him? Enough to agree to this kind of an arrangement, knowing the conclusion in advance? Would it be worth it?

Then she got the strange stirring deep in her pelvis simply from the memory of making love to him. Being with Ry was like having the earth shift beneath her feet, like fireworks, like nothing she'd ever experienced. Could she really let that go so soon?

"I'm not ready for it to be over either," she whispered. "I don't know what you do to me, Ry, but I'm not going to be satisfied with just tonight."

He shifted on the seat, scooting over to be closer to her. She turned her face up to his and he kissed her, long and deep.

"I love your honesty," he said, his lips by her ear. "I swear to God, it turns me on."

"You're crazy."

"You're just figuring that out now?" He nibbled on her earlobe, teasing.

If he wasn't careful, she was going to start climbing all over him again.

"You want to stay at the house tonight?" he asked, and to add a little persuasion, he slid his tongue down the tendon of her neck.

She shivered. "I'd better not tonight. I don't have a change of clothes, and my parents will wonder if I don't come home. Not that I need their permission, but I'd rather avoid that awkward conversation tomorrow morning."

"It's your house."

"And they know I haven't moved in yet." She touched her finger to the tip of his nose. "Don't be so impatient."

"Can you blame me? I just had my mind blown. I'd like for that to happen again." He winked at her. "As soon as possible."

"Tomorrow night," she suggested. "I'll bring a load of stuff over after dinner. It might take me a while to get back home again."

"It's a date."

They were doing this. Embarking on an affair. It was all terribly exciting, yet she couldn't quite rid herself of the nagging feeling that it wasn't going to turn out happily in the end. Would they be able to walk away unscathed?

Could she truly let go and just enjoy the moment for once?

Now that the steam was gone from the windows, Rylan put the truck in gear and they pulled a U-turn, headed back toward the main road and Gibson. The road was washed clean from the rain, and the sky was lightening to the west, little lines of peach and purple marking the sunset.

He dropped her off at home. Drops of rain still clung to the flowers and shrubs surrounding her porch. "Thanks for dinner," she said softly, picking up her purse. "I, uh, had a really nice time."

"Me, too, K. Me, too."

There was an awkward moment where she was undecided about whether or not to kiss him good-night. He put the truck in Park and faced her, his eyes twinkling.

"Is this one of those 'do we or don't we' moments?"

She laughed, her breath coming out in a soft, feminine sound she hadn't known she was capable of making. "Kind of," she replied.

"I vote for do. Then I can take the taste of your lips home with me."

Had she really called him charming earlier? It was more than that. Rylan knew how to be sweet. And if he wasn't sincere, he definitely had a knack of appearing convincing.

She leaned in partway, he did, too, and they kissed goodbye, a sweet, lingering kiss that ended with a soft parting of lips and a sigh. At least on her part.

"Good night, Kailey."

"Good night, Ry."

She opened her door and hopped out of the truck, then slid her purse strap over her shoulder. At the bottom of the porch steps she turned around and gave a little wave, and he lifted one finger off the steering wheel in a casual acknowledgment. Then he put the truck in gear and headed back out the driveway.

It turned out that having a relationship with Rylan wasn't as fraught with difficulty as she'd expected. Work on the ranches kept them busy during the day, and Rylan moved back to Crooked Valley after the single night they spent at her house. She wondered if it was because staying at her house would have felt a little too much like something permanent, but she tried not to dwell on it. For right now, living their own lives with their own purposes seemed to be working well.

Rylan's shoulder improved and his bruising faded, and he dutifully went to his physical therapy appointments, wanting to be completely healed and healthy to return to competition.

The haying was mostly finished for the season and on her visits to Crooked Valley, Kailey spent time with Carrie and little Evan, and helped Lacey in the kitchen during her first year of putting up garden harvest. Kailey had been doing it with her mom for years, so she spent fun evenings helping Lacey can tomatoes, green and yellow beans, carrots, beets and dill pickles. When they were done, she and Rylan often would go for a walk in the moonlight. Sometimes they'd miraculously end up at his camper, satisfying their hunger for each other that never seemed to go away.

One of Kailey's mares came into heat and they bred her to Rattler, hoping for a healthy foal the next summer. During a particularly hot dry spell, they met at the swimming hole after quitting time and made love in the cool, refreshing water, laughing at some of the awkward logistics but totally enamored with the feel of the cool water on their hot skin. Afterward, they lay on the grassy bank on soft towels, and Rylan made love to her again, slowly and thoroughly, so that when they parted ways she was sure she gave off a glow the whole way home.

In September, Brandt was taking a fair number of stock to a rodeo in Lewiston. The foreman who normally traveled with the stock was taking a little vacation since his wife had just had their fourth baby, so Kailey decided to make the trip herself. A few days before, she asked Rylan to go with her.

They were over at the Brandt spread, walking back from the east pasture when she put forth the invite.

"So…Lewiston coming up this week."

"Weather looks good. You're traveling with the crew?"

She nodded, but her heart was pounding like crazy. Why was she so nervous about asking him, anyway? "Have you missed it?"

"Missed what?" He looked over at her, his eyes shadowed from the sun by his hat.

Truth be told, she never got tired of looking at him. The sexy quirk to his lips, the strong jaw, the little bit of reddish-brown hair that curled just above his collar… Rylan Duggan was as sexy as they came.

"The show. I mean, you lived it every weekend up until a month ago." He'd stopped wearing his sling after the first two weeks, and was slowly working on getting strength and mobility back.

"I do," he confessed. "Don't get me wrong, working with the horses at home has been good. But yeah, I miss it." He grinned. "Maybe I have an addiction."

Just ask him, a voice in her head said.

"So…why don't you come with me? We're leaving Tuesday at noon and coming back Saturday night. It'll be busy, but you can take in the competition, see some of the guys, and I'll have some company other than Dan and Jim." She named the two hands who would be traveling with her. "Not that there's anything wrong with them, but, well, there's generally just chew, spitting and monosyllables."

He stopped and looked at her. "You're asking me to spend four nights with you in a motel?"

Her courage started to wither. "Too much?"

"I don't know."

At least he was being honest. She tried hard not to be disappointed, and most of the time she tried not to think about where their relationship was going or what was around the corner. But it was hard. She wanted to spend time with him…real time, not just sneaking in romantic rendezvous every few days.

"If it would make you more comfortable, I could book you your own room," she offered. "And you don't have to come. I just… thought I'd put the offer out there in case you wanted to get away for a few days." She offered a bright smile. No big deal.

"Kailey." He came up beside her again and took her hand. "Believe me, there is nothing I'd like more than four days locked up in a motel room with you."

She swallowed. That was how they'd started, after all. In a motel room. She actually hadn't thought of that until just now. But this wasn't February, it was September. And clearly this wasn't a one-night thing. They'd been seeing each other for weeks. Then again, if he went with her and stayed in the motel with her, their secret relationship wouldn't be so secret anymore.

"Well, think about it. The offer's open, but my feelings won't be hurt if you say no."

It was a complete lie, but she wanted it to be true. That should count for something, right?

"I'd like to go," he said, squeezing her hand. "You're right. I have missed the scene, a lot. It'll be strange not competing, but it'll be fun, too. And I can give you a hand now and again."

"Great," she said, relieved and a little bit excited. "Come over on Tuesday. The guys can take the trailers and I can drive with you, if that's okay."

"Sounds just fine," he agreed.

They were in sight of the house now and he dropped her hand. Kailey held back a sigh. At first the sneaking around had been exciting. Now, though, it was starting to feel old. Instead of a secret it was something different. Something…less. She discovered there was a big difference between wanting to keep something to yourself and wanting to keep it from other people.

"Thanks for the walk," she said, slowing her steps. "I suppose I should get inside and give Mom a hand. Her migraines have been acting up, and she's been trying to keep up with the last of the garden."

"Do you ever stop?" he asked. It wasn't a criticism. One thing she could say about Ry, he didn't seem threatened by her drive and work ethic. Maybe that came from being raised by a single mom who'd had to work hard to support her family.

"Occasionally," she replied.

They stopped by his truck and he opened the door. Before he hopped in, he pulled her close and kissed her, his soft lips melded to hers.

She wished she hadn't noticed that the truck and open door hid them from any eyes that might see what they were up to.

"G'night, beautiful," he said, hopping into the cab and throwing her a wink.

"Good night, Ry."

He drove off in a cloud of dust, leaving her standing in the yard.

She'd walked into this with her eyes wide open, so she couldn't expect too much. Instead she turned around and headed for the house, prepared to help her mom and keep busy so she didn't spend any more time thinking about what their relationship was… and wasn't.

Chapter 11

To say that Ry was having second thoughts
was a massive understatement.

He pulled into the Brandt yard, duffel bag
beside him on the seat, ready for four days
of rodeo and four nights with a beautiful
woman.

To anyone else, it had to look as if he had
life right by the tail.

To Ry, it was an uncomfortable realization
that he'd agreed to this even though he knew
it meant a giant step forward for their relationship. A relationship that was supposed to
be based solely on enjoying each other with
no plans beyond the here and now.

But even Rylan knew that you didn't spend four whole days with a woman without it meaning something.

The yard was a hive of activity. The hands were in the throes of loading stock into trailers, ready to make the drive to Lewiston. Kailey's dad was there, too, supervising alongside his daughter, who had her honey-streaked hair pulled up in a ponytail and sunglasses shading her eyes. She lifted her hand to her forehead as if the sun was in her way, and he accepted the truth: he was far more involved with Kailey Brandt than he'd ever wanted to be. Not far behind that little nugget of honesty was a second. It wasn't caring about her that was freaking him out. It was the fact that he *wasn't* freaking out about it that had him panicking.

He should just come up with a good excuse and make his apologies. They could distance themselves slowly, ease away from each other and just be friends again.

Then he thought of Kailey's sharp tongue and hot temper and realized that would never be an option. She was too much of a firecracker.

A smile bloomed on her face the moment she saw his truck, and he saw her lean over and say something to her dad. The senior Brandt had a stern face that Rylan couldn't read, but he could take a pretty good guess. Kailey was his only child and a daughter, no less.

He hopped out of the truck. "Looks like you're in the thick of it," he called out, crossing the yard.

"Nearly done. Jim's loading the bulls now. We should be on the road in the next thirty. Your timing's great."

They walked back over to where Mr. Brandt was standing with his arms folded across his chest. Formidable. Rylan couldn't help but respect him for it.

"Afternoon, Mr. Brandt." He held out his hand. "Good to see you again."

Brandt shook his hand, a firm grip that held just a little bit of threat. "Duggan. Heard you're traveling with this circus this afternoon."

"Yes, sir. The accident sidelined me and I have to confess, I've missed it. I'm looking forward to watching some events, lending a hand when I can."

Kailey had started chewing on a fingernail, but she dropped her hand as if she'd suddenly realized she was doing it. "Oh, Rylan, I booked your room for you."

"Thanks for looking after that," he said, understanding. Perhaps they weren't as far apart on this relationship thing as he thought. She was certainly making an effort to make it appear as though they weren't together.

There was a shout and Kailey trotted off to see what the fuss was about, leaving Rylan beside her dad.

"Rylan, I'm not a stupid man. I can see how things are."

"Yes, sir." He'd half expected to get some sort of "talk" this afternoon. Brandt wasn't going to beat around the bush. Rylan figured that was where Kailey got her direct nature.

"I don't need to say anything more, do I, son?"

Rylan shook his head. "No, sir. That's your little girl out there and she's also the person who's going to run this ranch. In other words, she's not a woman to trifle with."

"You might be smarter than I gave you credit for," Brandt said gruffly.

Rylan looked Kailey's father in the eye. "Begging your pardon, sir, but you know Kailey better than me. So I'm sure you know that she's made her wishes and thoughts crystal clear. She is one of the most forthright women I've ever known."

Brandt chuckled a little. "That doesn't scare you?"

"Of course not. Women are hard to understand. One who says exactly what she means? That's like breaking the secret code right there."

There was silence again as they both watched Kailey shut the trailer and latch it, then dust off her hands.

"Just for the record," Brandt said, his voice firm once again. "I'm not entirely happy about this situation."

"Yes, sir."

"But she's a grown woman. She's got to make her own choices and I respect that."

"Me, too," Rylan agreed.

"All right then," Brandt said.

A few minutes later the convoy was rolling out the yard, Kailey perched on Rylan's truck seat, her eyes alight with excitement. "So," she said, her tone a little too conversational to be natural. "You and my dad. Talk about anything interesting?"

Rylan looked over and then back at the road. "The weather."

"Right." She laughed a little. "Try again."

"Let's just say we understand each other and leave it at that."

"He's not going to show up at the motel tonight with a shotgun?"

Rylan shook his head. "I doubt it. After all, I'll be in my own room."

When Kailey didn't offer a smart remark, he glanced over at her. Damned if she wasn't blushing. "Kailey?"

She bit down on her lip. "Well, there isn't exactly another room. I just said that so Dad would think we weren't staying together."

He wasn't sure if he was relieved or disappointed. "You don't think his spies will fill him in the moment we get back?"

"Maybe, but then the trip's over and done with." Her grin flashed again. "If you asked him what I was like as a kid, he'd tell you I was a great one for asking forgiveness rather than permission."

"I bet."

"You want to share driving? We'll probably gas up in Missoula and then go straight through." She changed the subject.

"We'll see. I'm used to long drives, K. And I'm not even hauling anything this time. Six hours is nothing."

"Well, let me know then. It's a pretty drive. I haven't gone for a few years, but you can't beat it for scenery."

They were content not to talk for a long time. Instead the music on the radio and the sweeping foothills leading to the mountains kept them content. In Missoula they stopped for gas and a quick snack. Dinner would be later in the evening, as they'd have to get the stock settled before any of them could head to the motel for the night.

At one point Rylan looked over and realized that Kailey had fallen asleep, her head tipped to one side, bolstered a bit by the strap of the seat belt on her shoulder. She was so beautiful, but so wrapped up in the ranch and everything going on that he was pretty sure she didn't realize how incredible she was.

He had some decisions to make and soon. He was enjoying Crooked Valley more than he expected. In Wyoming, he'd been a hand on a cattle ranch. It had been good work and he'd had a great boss, but working with the rough stock at Crooked Valley was surprisingly fulfilling. He knew he'd told Duke that he would stay on until Christmas so that the terms of the will would be fulfilled, but the thought of leaving the ranch made him feel a little bit empty inside. Who would care for Rattler and the other horses? Where would he be next summer when Candyfloss foaled? Quinn was doing an okay job, but he'd been happy to leave the decisions to Rylan, saying a smart man played to his strengths and acknowledged his weaknesses. Plus, with Carrie and Duke starting a family, Quinn was taking on more of Carrie's foreman duties.

And then there was the woman sleeping beside him. This was the longest he'd ever stayed with anyone. He'd gotten very good at picking out women who were only out for a good time so he could avoid romantic complications. That hadn't worked with Kailey. He was in it up to his neck.

And finally, there was the rodeo. It was in his blood. He couldn't deny that he was looking forward to the next few days because being on the fairgrounds, listening to conversations, smelling the food booths' savory offerings and watching the events would feel like being home. Heck, it had been his home for the past few years.

Kailey woke up about a half hour from Lewiston. He figured she must have been tired from the long work days. Once she rubbed her eyes her energy was renewed and she was raring to go. "Oh, my gosh. We're almost there! I slept a long time."

"Yes, you did. Missed the prettiest part, too. But I didn't have the heart to wake you."

She smiled. "There's always the drive back."

They made it to the fairgrounds in good time, and everyone worked together to get the stock unloaded and cared for for the night. When Kailey told Dan and Jim she'd hang around for a while to make sure things were okay, they shook their heads.

"No, ma'am," Jim said. "One of us will do that. We all usually take turns anyway, and I ain't got a damned thing going on tonight."

"You arguing with the boss, Jim?"

Rylan chuckled down low. Jim had to know that was a battle he'd lose.

"No, ma'am. Just suggesting you enjoy tonight 'cause it's gonna get real busy around here." Rylan figured Kailey had been right about the chew when Jim spat off to the side. "You and Rylan should go get a nice dinner or something."

That she didn't automatically contradict him surprised Rylan. Finally she gave a shrug. "You're sure?"

"Sure I'm sure. We can handle things. We would've if you hadn't come, wouldn't we?"

"Yes, I guess you would. Everything's taken care of at the motel. I guess I'll see you in the morning."

"Yes, ma'am." Jim had done the talking, but Dan touched the brim of his hat and grinned.

They were back in Rylan's truck and Kailey frowned. "You really think everything's okay?"

Rylan laughed. "Gosh, you really haven't traveled with the crew in a while, have you? Look, they'll make sure everything's fine and then they'll grab a few beers and head back to the motel. Could be that having the boss lady along is cramping their style a bit."

She looked at him, her worry deepening the crease between her eyes. "Hey," he added, "that doesn't mean they won't do their jobs. It just means that they'll be extra careful about being well-behaved. You're their boss. And you're a lady. There are... sensibilities."

She snorted. "Rylan, I've been working with ranch hands since I started walking. I think I've heard it all."

"Yep," he agreed. "And those men respect

you. So they'll step up and go the extra mile for you this week. You didn't have to come along. You could have sent someone else. But they know that they work with you, not just for you. And I'm guessing they admire that about you a lot."

He knew he did. She was some woman. Tough and strong when she needed to be, and soft and tender, too.

"So, where do you want to go to eat? Any ideas? I'm starving."

They ended up heading through town and stopping at a Mexican place, but instead of sitting to eat, they ordered takeout, stopped for a six-pack of beer, and took it all back to the motel. Kailey insisted she was too dirty and smelly to be in polite company, and what she really wanted was some chow and a hot shower. That suited Ry just fine, and before long they were checked into their room and sitting at the little table with takeout trays of enchiladas and Spanish rice spread over the top and two semi-cold beers ready to wash it all down.

After their messy but tasty meal, Kailey disappeared into the bathroom for a hot shower and Rylan shoved all their garbage into a paper bag and put it in the waste basket. He cracked open another beer and parted the curtains, staring out the window at his truck parked in front of the room and the rather dreary lot across from the motel. He still wasn't convinced he should have said yes to the trip. In all his years of traveling to rodeos and fairs he'd managed to stay free of the relationship trap. Sometimes he'd indulged in what was offered, sometimes not, but never had he let his heart get involved. And never had he given any woman false hope for the future. He was terrified that that was what he was doing right now. And hurting Kailey was the last thing he ever wanted to do.

She came out of the bathroom, letting out a cloud of steam and floral scent. He turned around and his fingers tightened around his beer. She was wrapped in one of the motel's white towels, nothing more, her wet hair slicked back from her face like a mermaid's.

He shut the curtains.

She was fresh-faced, radiant, devoid of makeup or perfect hair. Just a woman in a towel. He swallowed, his throat thick with truth. Not just a woman. His woman. He'd been trying to deny it for some time now, but it was no use. He was falling for her and hard. She was going to make leaving Crooked Valley so difficult, but he wasn't going to think about that right now. Couldn't. Right now there was just her, and him, and eight hours before they had to be up and at the roundup.

Kailey turned the top on her bottle of water and took a long swig. Early September could be cool or it could be blistering hot and today it was hot. She could see the waves of heat shimmering in the air as competition got under way in the afternoon. Today one of their bulls, Brandt's Boilermaker, would be in the lineup. This was the first year they'd put Boiler in the arena, and so far he'd done well. She had her fingers crossed for an exciting show today.

Rylan came up beside her carrying two hot dogs. "Hey, you've got to eat. I brought some more water, too." A bottle bulged out the left chest pocket of his shirt. "It's a hot one for sure."

"Thanks," she answered, taking the hot dog and giving him a smile. Rylan had been different the past few days. Sometimes she got the feeling he was distant, as though his mind was somewhere else. But then other times she was the center of his focus. She'd never felt as cherished or loved as she had these past nights. There was a care in his lovemaking that hadn't been there before. The fire still burned as hot as ever, but there was more, and she knew she was falling in love with him.

In her head she knew she should stop. That it was no good. But then another sort of logic reminded her that you couldn't just dictate feelings and turn them on and off. They were what they were. And with the change in Rylan…well, maybe he was feeling it, too. Maybe they stood a chance…if they just took it slowly.

"You having fun?" she asked after chewing and swallowing a mouthful of bun.

"I am. It sucks being up here instead of down there." He nodded toward the chutes. "But it's fun to watch, too, and not have to worry about competing." He balled up his napkin. "I kinda miss the prize money, too, but what's done is done. I can't change it. Might as well accept it."

He took a big drink of water. "Besides, it's been kind of fun, working with the stock back home. I like it better than what I was doing before."

That was good, wasn't it? There were still a couple of months left before the anniversary of Joe's death. Maybe Rylan would change his mind. Stay on. He still could compete next year, when he was back in shape. And since that night at the hospital, he'd never once mentioned his leave-by date. He'd only talked about the business and his ideas for it.

"You've started implementing some good strategies," Kailey agreed. "Have you had any requests for Rattler's DNA? That would help your bottom line a lot."

He nodded. "I've been talking to a few people here that I know. To be honest, they were just sort of polite about it. Until I mentioned where I got Rattler and that we'd already bred him to one of Brandt's mares. That made their ears perk up a bit. I hope that's okay. I know I'm just along to enjoy the rodeo…"

"Don't be silly." She smiled over at him. "You'd be foolish not to take advantage of connections while you're here. Wasn't that one of the reasons you wanted my help to begin with?"

He nodded, then reached over and

squeezed her hand. "I just didn't want you to think I was using you," he said.

His low voice made everything in her go warm and squishy. "Of course not." The announcer called the next event and she nudged his arm. "Bull riding's about to start. Boilermaker's in this round."

They watched the events together. Kailey didn't go down to check on the guys until things were winding up for the day. She'd learned very quickly that not only were Jim and Dan fully capable, but the smartest thing for her to do was to step back and trust them to do their jobs. She stepped in when needed, and was always around to answer questions, and she also had a good chat with the on-site veterinarian. But mostly she enjoyed the week, the energetic atmosphere and being with Rylan.

Thursday night's dinner was take-out pizza. They'd started to enjoy taking their meal back to the motel, where they could kick off their boots and chill with a beer after the hot, dry days. Kailey looked at Ry over her slice and felt a wave of love wash over her. There was no denying it. She was in love with Rylan. No turning back, no reasoning it away. She loved how he looked, how he smiled, the way he teased his sister, the way he was patient with Amber, how he sat a horse and how he cared far more about things than he ever let on.

"What?" he asked, putting down his pizza and wiping his fingers on a napkin.

"Just this," she murmured, getting up from the chair. She went to him and he turned to face her, an expectant look on his perfect face. She put her hands on his shoulders and leaned down for a hot, searing kiss.

"Miss Brandt," he whispered. "I do declare."

"Declare what?" she asked, nibbling on his bottom lip. She heard the sharp intake of his breath.

"Declare that you're about to seduce me."

"You could be right."

A smile spread across his face, an expression of delight and with that ever-present teasing light to his eyes. "By all means," he said, sitting back in the chair. "I'm most willing to be seduced."

Another thing about Rylan. He was perfectly okay with not always being the one in control.

Slowly, as slowly as she could stand it, she slipped the buttons out of the holes of his shirt, then pushed the fabric off his shoulders. His chest was broad and strong, with a small swatch of reddish brown hair at the base of his neck and around his nipples. She unbuttoned the cuffs and slid the sleeves off his arms, then dropped the shirt on the floor without taking her eyes off his face. She loved him, wanted to kiss him everywhere, but she knew the number one way to drive him crazy was to show him what was in store.

So she stood just out of his reach, and slipped off her jeans. Then she unbuttoned her shirt, dropped it to the floor, and stood before him in a pale pink lace bra and a matching pair of bikinis that didn't really cover much of anything.

"Kailey," he uttered, his voice hoarse as he sat up straight in his chair.

But she took a step backward, letting him know it wasn't quite time. Instead she reached behind her back, undid the bra and let it fall down her arms to the floor. The panties followed suit, until she was naked before him.

Her gaze met his. Not just naked. Bare. In every way she could be without actually saying the words.

Slowly he got up from the chair. Took the two steps required to stand in front of her, but still he didn't touch her. He waited, as if he knew this time was for her, and she saw his chest rise and fall with the effort of standing perfectly still.

She reached for the waistband of his jeans. Undid it, then the zipper, then knelt and slid them down his legs until he could step out of them. Only his shorts remained, and she let her hand brush strategically against them before grabbing the waistband and disposing of them to the growing pile of clothing on the floor.

She reached for his hand. Lifted it, kissed it and placed it on her breast.

It was silent permission, and for long moments they kissed and touched until Kailey was sure she couldn't stand much longer. They moved to the bed, but if she'd thought things would move faster now, she was greatly mistaken. With more care and tenderness than she thought possible, Rylan made love to her so thoroughly her body hummed with satisfaction and her heart was so full she thought it might overflow.

She looked up at him, braced above her, and felt tears gather in the corners of her eyes. The words sat on her tongue but she couldn't bring herself to say them, too afraid they would ruin everything.

So she said them in her heart instead, wondering if he could feel them through their connection.

I love you, Rylan. I love you.

Chapter 12

She lay asleep beside him, naked between the plain white sheets, her hair spread on the pillow like a gold wave of summer wheat.

He was wide awake.

Rylan was still reeling from what had happened. From the moment she'd abandoned her food and walked over to where he'd been sitting, something had been different. Electric. It had just been...more.

Seeing her undress, offer herself like that to him, it had shaken him to the core, both sexually and emotionally. Until tonight he hadn't known what it really was to make love, but when they'd come together that was exactly what it had been. Love. Not just bodies but hearts.

God help him.

He turned onto his side and watched her sleep, reached out and tucked a piece of hair behind her ear so it didn't fall over her face. How had this happened?

Yet he'd known it was possible. Of course he had, in his hesitation to even come here with her this week. Things had been getting a little too comfortable. Too serious. It had been like this from the beginning. He'd just been pretending otherwise.

He loved her. It scared him to death. Almost as much as it scared him to think about staying at Crooked Valley indefinitely. Making that commitment to Lacey and Duke and investing so much of himself in any one single thing went against everything he had wanted for himself.

He sighed. But Kailey never moved. He'd discovered she was an incredibly sound sleeper. In the mornings he almost had to shake her awake since she merely slapped away at the snooze button on the clock radio, all without waking.

In the silence of the night there was a buzzing sound.

He reached over to the nightstand and grabbed his phone, frowning at the lit display. It was definitely his that was buzzing, and the number that came up was Duke's.

He slid out of bed and scooted into the bathroom to answer.

"Hello?"

"Rylan?"

"Carrie?"

"Yeah. I'm sorry to bother you, but…"

It was after midnight. If that weren't reason enough, something in her voice sent warning bells screaming through his head. "What's wrong?"

"It's Rattler. There's…been an accident."

His stomach seemed to plummet clear to his feet. "What happened?"

Carrie's voice was shaky. "We think it was a mountain lion. The vet's out here now, but I thought you ought to know."

He sat on the edge of the tub and pinched the bridge of his nose. Seventeen grand. The hopes for the whole program at Crooked Valley. But more than that, he felt sick at the thought of the pain and fear his horse was going through. "How bad," he breathed.

"Bad enough." She choked up a little. "Duke's with him now. They've got him sedated." He heard her gulp. "I've never heard a horse scream like that in my life."

There was nothing else to do. He had to head back to the ranch…tonight. As it was, he wouldn't make it back until early morning, and that was driving straight through. But Rattler was his horse. He was the biggest investment they'd put into the ranch and his responsibility, not Duke's or Quinn's.

"I'm coming back," he said to Carrie. "Go ahead and do what needs to be done to help him, okay? I'll hit the road in the next thirty."

"You're sure?"

"I'm sure. It's not like I'm competing or anything. This is more important. Tell Duke I'll see him as soon as I can."

"Okay, Rylan. Whatever you say."

He hung up, feeling slightly surprised at Carrie's response. *Whatever you say.* As if he was in charge of anything…

He ran his hand through his hair. He'd think of that later. Right now he had to get his stuff together and get going.

As Kailey slept on, he packed up his jeans and shirts and toiletries, shoved a few pieces of forgotten pizza in a paper bag and grabbed an unopened bottle of cola, thinking he could use the caffeine hit on the road. When he was all ready to leave, he went to the side of the bed and sat on the edge.

"Kailey," he said gently, putting a hand on her bare shoulder.

Nothing. He smiled softly, loving this little quirk about her. The woman, as she was about everything else, was serious about sleeping. Efficient. He gave her shoulder a little shake. "Kailey, wake up."

"Mmm," she murmured, but that was it. She rolled away from him and let out a deep breath.

"Kailey," he said again, but nothing.

He could really press matters and wake her. But she looked so soft and peaceful he didn't have the heart to do it. Still, he couldn't just leave. Not after what had happened between them before.

He grabbed the complimentary motel notepad and pen and wrote out a quick message.

K, there's been an accident with Rattler and I had to rush back to Crooked Valley. I'm sorry to leave in the night but it doesn't look good and it's my job to look after him. If you can't get a ride back with the guys call me and I'll come back to get you on Saturday night. I'm so sorry…thanks for this week. It's been amazing.

He hesitated over how to sign it. In the end he decided on a breezy, See you soon, Ry.

He ripped the sheet off the tablet and propped it up against the lamp on the dresser next to his room key. He shouldered his bag, grabbed the packet of pizza and gave her one last, lingering look, imprinting the image of her sleeping face on his mind before opening the door.

A cold front had come in during the evening and the stiff breeze that came with it caught the door, nearly pulling it from his hand. He stepped outside and then closed the door as gently as he could, hoping the sudden gust hadn't awakened Kailey. Seconds later he was in his truck, his bag on the seat beside him, backing out of the parking space and making his way through town to the highway that would take him home.

Kailey rolled over, squinted at the clock radio beside the bed. Seven forty? Surely Rylan would have gotten her up by now?

And then she realized that the other side of the bed was empty. And had been for some time. The sheets were cool.

"Ry?"

The shower wasn't running. And it didn't sound as though anyone was in there, either. Kailey was in the motel room all alone.

She crawled out of bed stark naked and hastily pulled on underwear and a shirt from a pile on the floor. She peeked through the curtains and saw that his truck was gone. Maybe he'd been up early and had just run out for some breakfast. He'd come back with coffee and sausage biscuits, and it would all be okay. She'd be a little late to the roundup but it would be fine.

She had a quick shower and dressed and when she came out of the bathroom he still wasn't back. A little beat of warning pulsed through her brain.

And then she realized his bag was gone. And so was his toothbrush and shampoo and anything that said Rylan Duggan had been here. It was seriously as if…he hadn't been there at all. All except the room key card, left propped up against the base of the lamp on the dresser.

He'd run.

The first sensation she felt was numbness, taking over her whole body, including her brain. For a few minutes the only words that would form in her head were *not again*. He wouldn't, couldn't have snuck out in the middle of the night as he had the last time, could he?

Could he?

She shoved her bottom back on the bed, pulled her knees up to her chest. Oh God. Oh God oh God oh God. Her breath started coming fast and shallow, her heart beat fast. She wouldn't panic. She'd hold herself together.

Only she couldn't. Because the last time it had just been one night. One single night, not weeks of caring for each other, not months. In February she hadn't been *in love* with him.

Like she was now.

Oh God.

Like she was now.

The tears she didn't want came anyway, streaking down her cheeks, forced out by sobs that choked her throat. "Why?" she cried softly, dropping her head to her knees. Why now? Why did he have to leave without a word in the middle of the night like a coward? Why did he have to break her heart just when she'd decided to trust him with it?

All the while the room key stared at her, accusing her of being a fool. Not just once, which had been difficult enough, but twice now. With the same man. The man who'd told her he was not permanent. Who'd made it clear from the beginning that he was just passing through.

Just who was the idiot here?

That was them. The idiot and the...she filled in the blank under her breath, the initial numbing pain transitioning to righteous anger.

He'd left her in a motel room six hours from home. When everyone knew he was there with her this week.

She thought of his face last night as he'd held her in his arms. He'd looked deeply into her eyes. Whispered her name. She'd been so sure. So very sure that this was a giant step forward for them. That he felt the same way for her as she did for him. Remembering that moment caused something deep inside her to shrivel up and die.

For some reason, men loved her. But they didn't ever love her enough. She was never their everything. Their reason for breathing.

The light in the darkness. Not like the way Quinn looked at Lacey. Or the way Duke smiled at Carrie as she held their baby son.

Kailey fell back among the sheets and finally let it out. All the disillusionment, the heartache, the humiliation and pain. She cried into the sheets until she was spent.

When she finally blinked her painful eyelids, she checked her watch. Eight-thirty. She couldn't show up like this. She had to get herself together. First thing to do was text Jim and let him know she was running late, ask if there was anything urgent and she'd catch up with him in a bit. She frowned and decided she'd pick up some doughnuts and coffee on the way as a peace offering.

Next she got out of bed and went to the bathroom, ran a sink of cold water, retrieved a washcloth from the towel bar and laid the cool cloth over her face, hoping to minimize the redness and puffiness. What she really wanted to do was collapse on Carrie's sofa with a bottle of wine and bawl out her troubles.

But Carrie didn't live in her little house anymore, and it felt awkward crying on her shoulder now that she was married with a family of her own. Lives changed...

At least some did. Some didn't, even when a girl tried.

She let the cold water work before patting her face dry and surveying the damage. It wasn't pretty. Defiantly she reached for her makeup bag. She usually didn't wear much to the rodeo grounds, but desperate times called for desperate measures. The only way she could get through today…and tomorrow…was to put Rylan Duggan at the back of her mind. Not spare him a single thought. She was Kailey Brandt, general manager of Brandt Ranch. Strong and capable. Maybe she'd been stupid to chafe against her commitment there, because one thing she could say about the ranch: never once had it let her down.

Moisturizer, concealer, foundation, powder. She used them all to smooth out her complexion, and then added a swipe of clear lip gloss and a coat of mascara on her lashes.

She examined herself in the mirror. Not perfect, but perhaps fixed enough that it looked as if she'd not had much sleep versus a ginormous crying jag over a man who wasn't worth it.

She scowled. "You are not going to think

about him," she instructed her reflection in a stern voice.

The other issue right now was transportation. She'd traveled with Rylan, and the guys were already gone, so she'd have to find another way to the rodeo grounds.

Her lower lip quivered in a moment of weakness; she bit it and stopped the trembling.

Rylan's key sat defiantly on the dresser and she left it there. This time she wouldn't deliver his key or anything else to the motel office. It could damn well sit there until the end of the world for all she cared.

The taxi she'd called arrived and stoically she got inside, gave the address to the driver and prepared herself to face the day.

Rylan Duggan was not the end of the world.

She wouldn't let him be.

The rest of the rodeo seemed to drag on twice as long as the first two days. Kailey let go of her hands-off approach and dug in and worked side by side with Jim and Dan, getting her boots and hands dirty. Friday night she went back to the room and took a long bath and opened a bottle of wine she'd grabbed when Jim had stopped for some beer on the way back to the motel. Normally she wasn't for self-medicating, but she could still smell Rylan in the room and she shifted between anger and sadness depending on the moment. Three glasses in she brushed her teeth and crawled beneath the sheets, hoping for eight hours of oblivion. Tomorrow afternoon they had a horse in the finals, and after that they'd be packing up and making the long drive home, arriving sometime close to midnight. The idea of being home in her own bed was soothing. She only had to make it twenty-four hours and she could stop this pretense.

The only person who'd asked about Rylan had been Jim. Dan was working away behind him and Jim had asked where Rylan was. She'd tried to keep her expression and voice neutral as she explained briefly that Rylan had needed to return to Crooked Valley, and would Jim mind if she hitched a ride back with him? He couldn't exactly say no, and she wasn't about to share personal details with an employee, no matter how friendly they all were.

On Saturday morning Kailey was up and ready to go by seven-thirty, and she and Jim drove to the grounds together. Her heart was still hurting, and she was still angrier than she ever remembered being. But she was holding it together. At some point she'd let everything out, but not now. She let the anger feed her composure until she was a model of efficiency and straight-up business.

The finals began right after lunch and Kailey put her personal feelings aside and focused on Lucifer, their bareback entry into the competition. He was smaller than Crooked Valley's Rattler, and compact, well-suited to bareback competition and with a glistening jet-black coat that made him a treat to watch.

When the time came, he was loaded into the chute, his hooves stomping as he tossed his mane. The cowboy who'd drawn him was a twenty-five-year-old out of Oklahoma who had the highest score going into the final. Kailey crossed her fingers as she waited for the door to open. A good ride for both cowboy and horse would mean good things. Brandt stock was in demand; Kailey wanted to keep it that way.

The horn sounded, the chute opened and horse and rider burst into the arena. Lucifer lived up to his name, bucking like the devil, throwing in a few turns and twists trying to unseat his rider. Eight seconds later it was all over, with a clean ride and the wait for final points. When the board lit up, Kailey grinned from ear to ear. An eighty-seven… a damned good mark, and good scoring for both competitors.

Lucifer was their last competitor, so Kailey took a long breath and exhaled it. She wished they could simply load up and leave right now, since their part of the competition was over. But Jim and Dan had spent the whole week following standings and performances. The extra hour and a bit to let them watch the finals wasn't too much to ask.

One good thing about it was that they'd checked out of the motel that morning. For the first time since he left, Kailey had picked up Rylan's key card, only to return it to the main office with her own. Her bag was in Jim's truck. The dried-up pizza and box were in the trash and she could start putting this behind her. For good. She'd given Rylan a second chance, but she wouldn't be giving him a third.

The bull-riding had just started when her phone buzzed. Surprised, she immediately pulled it out of her back pocket and looked at the screen. A text message…from Rylan. In a split second she went from surprise to traitorous excitement to red-hot anger at his presumption that a text message would be an acceptable form of communication at this point.

You coming home tonight?

What the heck? He'd left her high and dry and then wanted to know when she was getting home? As if nothing had happened? Lips pursed, she shoved the phone back into her pocket, leaving the text unanswered.

It buzzed again. And once more when the third competitor was having the ride of his life. She blindly took the phone out and shut off the power. She was not going to give him the satisfaction of an answer. If they talked at all, it would be at a time and place of her choosing. It would be when she decided what she wanted to say and not before. She definitely wasn't going to engage in a text argument when they needed to speak face-to-face. She wasn't going to be a coward and take the easy way out. Not like he had.

The rodeo finally ended and Kailey headed straight for the truck, ready to load their stock on the trailer and make the long ride home.

Right now, that was all that mattered.

Chapter 13

Rylan checked his phone one more time and frowned.

Six. Six text messages since yesterday afternoon and she hadn't answered a single one. Plus two phone calls that had gone straight to voice mail. He had moments of worrying about her but then told himself she was with Jim and Dan and if anything were wrong, someone would be aware of it. So he worried that she was angry at him for leaving, though he'd explained everything in his note.

Surely, she could understand his needing to come home during an emergency.

He rubbed his hand over the stubble on his chin, realized he hadn't shaved since Thursday morning. It was nearly a beard, and he should probably take the time now that he knew Rattler was going to be okay.

For whatever reason, she wasn't answering his calls, and he was getting tired of it. His patience wasn't endless, and he dialed the number one more time, willing her to answer.

Straight to voice mail.

He ran his hand through his hair and stared at the wall of his camper. When the tone sounded, he left a message. "Kailey, I don't know why you're not answering your calls or texts, but I'm starting to get annoyed. Please call me back. Clearly we need to talk."

He hung up, knowing deep down she wouldn't call. But now he was really spooled up and he dialed the other number he knew now by heart: the main line at the Brandt ranch.

Her mother answered the phone.

"Good morning, Mrs. Brandt. How're you? It's Rylan Duggan."

There was a disapproving pause. "Hello, Rylan. What can I do for you?"

You can tell your pigheaded daughter to start answering her messages, he thought irritably, but instead he forced his voice to be pleasant. "I was just wondering if everyone made it back from Lewiston okay."

"Sure did. Rolled in around eleven-thirty last night."

He was relieved…and then annoyed all over again. "Is Kailey there?"

"I'm sorry, but she went home after they finished up here. I'll tell her you called."

In a pig's eye, he thought. As he hung up the call, he frowned and felt like kicking something. Dammit, the Brandts were ranchers. If they couldn't understand him leaving to take care of his own stock in an emergency…

He thought back to the note he'd left in the motel room along with his key. Had he not explained things sufficiently? Maybe if she'd pick up her stupid phone or answer a text, he could clear things up.

But the truth slapped him in the face. Kailey didn't want to clear things up. If she had she'd be over here talking. Asking him what had happened. But she wasn't. She was acting as if he didn't even exist.

And to think he'd fancied himself falling in love with her.

He flopped back on the bed, put his hands behind his head. That was the problem, wasn't it? He'd gone and done the one thing he hadn't wanted to do. He'd fallen in love. It had been coming for a while now, but last Thursday night had really cemented it. It had been different. All his barriers had been broken down when he looked into her eyes. Hell, he'd almost told her he loved her.

He was glad now he hadn't.

When he was sure he'd wallowed enough, he headed to the house for the breakfast he'd missed. Lacey was in the kitchen, pouring Quinn a midmorning cup of coffee now that Amber had gone off to school for the day. Quinn took one look at him and raised an eyebrow. "Wow. You do not look like you're in a good mood."

"I'm not, particularly," he answered, opening the fridge. "Lace, you got any leftovers I can heat up or something?"

"For breakfast? Sit down. I'll get you something."

"I can make my own."

"I know that. But I'll be faster. And you

can get some coffee in your system. Maybe that'll help your sour mood."

She elbowed him aside and he stomped to the cupboard for a mug. In no time at all she'd fried up a piece of ham, sliced up a potato for home fries, and had made him a couple of fried eggs. Quinn hadn't said much as all this was going on, but when Ry finally sat down with his plate of food, Quinn pushed away his cup and sat back in his chair.

"Everything okay with Rattler?"

Ry nodded and sliced into the flavorful ham. "He's doing better. Some of those gashes are going to be a long time healing. No permanent damage, though, I don't think."

"Good. Lucky, too. Everyone's on alert now. For a cat to come this close…you have to be on the lookout. Especially with kids and pets."

Rylan nodded again. "You have trouble with cats before?"

Quinn shook his head. "Not so much. Last winter it was coyotes."

"We didn't much either at the last place I was at." Rylan finished his eggs and sat back. "Much as I hate to say it, if it's not captured…"

"I know," Quinn replied, his face solemn. "None of us likes the alternative."

Rylan got up and took his plate to the sink. "Thanks for breakfast, sis."

"Anytime, Ry." Lacey smiled at him. "I like having you around."

He jostled her elbow, a gesture of brotherly teasing, and then turned to Quinn. "You got a few minutes? There's something I want to run past you."

"Sure. I'll walk with you down to the barn."

The air was cooler in the mornings now, and some of the leaves were beginning to turn a telltale gold that marked the advent of autumn. It was one of Rylan's favorite times of year, when the heat was less brash and the colors of everything—the sky, the grass— seemed more vivid. He let out a big breath.

"Something on your mind, Ry? And I don't think this has anything to do about Rattler."

Since Kailey wasn't answering his texts, he figured one of her best friends might be a help. Particularly a guy friend. "So…Kailey's not answering my texts or taking my calls."

"What did you do?"

"I don't know. I came back here, but..." He wondered how open to be and figured he didn't have much to lose. "I didn't wake her before I left. I tried, but I swear a freight train could've gone through the room and she would've slept right through it. Instead I left my key and I wrote her a note explaining what had happened."

Quinn nodded. "A good note?"

"I thought so. I mean, I don't think I left anything out."

"And what happened?"

They stopped outside the corral, watched a group of mares standing in the sun, their hides flat and gleaming. "That's just it," he replied. "Nothing happened. I was so busy with Rattler and then so tired that it wasn't until Saturday morning that I realized she hadn't called or even sent a text to see how things were. And when I tried to reach her... no answer. I even tried calling her folks' place this morning and they put me off. What do I do, Quinn? Do I go over there? Or do I wait?"

Quinn looked over at him, his lips curved

up the slightest bit on one side of his mouth. "You got it bad, Rylan?"

"The worst," he confirmed readily. "Swore I wouldn't. Couldn't. But there it is. I promised you I wouldn't mess with her, Quinn, and I haven't. I love her."

"I'm glad to hear it. You're a good man, Rylan. I don't pretend to understand all your motivations for how you've lived your life, but I know a good guy when I see one."

"Then what do I do? What's your read on the situation?"

The semi-smile slid off Quinn's lips. "I think that even if Kailey says she forgives you for February, it's always going to be in the back of her mind. And you leaving her in another motel room is probably hitting her right where it hurts. Even if you did have a good reason."

"But not to answer a single text? I don't get it. I mean, aren't women supposed to be all about the talking? The silent treatment is freaking me out."

Quinn frowned. "Ry, figuring out why women do anything is a mystery man will probably never solve. But maybe she chose the silent treatment because she knew it would freak you out. Maybe this is her way of showing you how it felt. I don't know, man. But you should talk. If you love her, you have to try."

"I think so, too. I think I was just hoping she'd come to me, you know?"

Quinn grinned. "You wanted her to make it easy on you? Oh, brother, you picked the wrong woman for that. But after knowing Kailey for a lot of years, I can tell you that she's worth it. Don't throw in the towel yet."

Ry felt marginally better, but he spent the better part of the day alternately checking his phone and pondering how exactly he should approach her. At the ranch? At Quinn's house? Ask her over here? What would he say?

Would he be welcome or walking into a rattlesnake's nest?

In the end Quinn was the one who came up with the solution. He knocked on Rylan's camper door around seven and stuck his head inside when Ry called out.

"Hey, Ry? Kailey just called. She said there's something going on with the washing machine and wondered if I'd take a look."

"Really?" Ry met Quinn's eyes. "Kailey seems the type that could handle a repair on her own."

Quinn's eyes glinted with humor. "I agree. I'm guessing she wants to ask me the same questions you did this morning. I was thinking I'd send you instead. Cut out the middle man."

Rylan thought for a minute. He wanted to talk to her. Needed to, but he was scared, too. Like he was walking into unknown territory full of traps.

"I guess I can do that."

"Take a toolbox. Look official, and say I sent you because I was busy."

"You think she'll buy that?"

Quinn chuckled. "Not a chance."

He ducked out again, then popped back in with one last encouragement. "Good luck, Ry."

Even though it was just for show, Rylan shoved a little handyman box he kept for simple repairs into the truck. He considered having a second shower but then decided he didn't need to procrastinate and instead changed into a clean shirt and ran a comb through his hair.

The drive seemed to take hours rather than a few minutes.

Kailey's truck was in the yard and the butterflies in Rylan's gut went from fluttering to ferocious. She mattered. No one had mattered this much to him for as long as he could remember. He really didn't want to screw this up.

Heart in his throat, he got out of the truck, grabbed his toolbox and headed for her front door.

She met him on the step, standing in front of the doorway to prevent him from entering. "I sent for Quinn. My landlord," she emphasized.

He kept his voice even, though seeing her right now both thrilled him and scared him to death. She'd clearly showered earlier, because her hair was soft and damp and smelled like the shampoo he now recognized, and she was wearing sweats and a soft hoodie. She looked utterly snuggly.

"Quinn said to tell you he's busy and that whatever you need fixed, to have me take a look at it."

She frowned. Sighed. Which might have been bad enough but then he looked her in the eye and what he saw startled him. Finality. And he didn't understand why.

"There's nothing wrong with the washer. I made that up. You can go home now."

His patience was thin, but he told himself to keep calm, try to get to the bottom of what had created such a change. "See, the thing is, Quinn figured you wanted to talk. And since I already put him in the middle today asking his advice…he figured he'd just get out of the way." Rylan tried a small smile, attempting to soften that hard look that she kept giving him.

"And what did Quinn say?"

There was a sarcastic edge to her words that Rylan didn't much care for. "He said he'd never been able to figure out women. He really wasn't much help."

"And do you need help, Rylan?"

Anger, so much anger in her tone. And pain, too. He heard bits of it bleeding through her words and he reminded himself to be patient. To get to the bottom of what was going on without losing his cool.

"Kailey, what happened? Why are you so angry? You didn't answer any of my texts and phone calls… I know I left in a hurry, but Rattler was in a real state and I had to get back as soon as I could."

Her mouth dropped open. "Angry? Why am I angry? Are you serious?" Her voice lifted and Rylan looked around. The next house was a couple of acres away, and normally that would be lots of privacy. But not if Kailey really let loose.

"Of course I'm serious," he replied carefully. "K, we're talking about you and me here. That's something I take very seriously."

She burst out laughing, but not the amused kind. The harsh, incredulous kind that was like knives. "Rylan, one thing I can say for sure. You don't ever take anything seriously."

Well. Now he knew what she really thought about him, didn't he? And it stung. More than he expected it would.

She shook her head, as if she couldn't believe what he'd said. "What was I supposed to think, when I woke up again and you were gone? Not only gone, but you left me high and dry with no vehicle. Six hours from home. You know what, Ry? Fool me once, shame on you. But fool me twice? That's shame on me. I should never have given you a second chance."

The words whipped at him and for a moment he was so stunned he didn't know what to say. When he finally figured it out, he gave back as good as he got. Because she was accusing him of something he didn't do.

"Fool you? For God's sake, Kailey. Rattler nearly died from that attack and he's my responsibility. Mine. I couldn't expect Quinn and Duke to just handle things when I wasn't even competing. I was along for the ride last week. Enjoying the time with you. I was needed at home."

"You could have just explained that!" she shouted.

"I did!" he shouted back. He tempered his voice a little. "I did and you know it. I explained it all in the note I left with the key card on the desk."

"What note?"

His heart froze. "What do you mean, what note? I tried to wake you up, but you're a sound sleeper. So I wrote you a note and put it by the lamp, right by my key. I explained that Rattler got attacked and was really injured. That I was heading back home to take care of things, but that I'd come to get you on Saturday if you needed me to. And when I texted you, I got nothing. I tried to call you, and it went right to voice mail."

"There wasn't any note, Rylan," she snapped. "And you expect me to believe you got this sudden attack of accountability?" She laughed.

He was starting to get worked up. "You know what? I get damned sick of people telling me how irresponsible I am. How I don't care about anything. I made a pretty big investment in Crooked Valley and he's my horse. Would you have rather I didn't care enough to look after him? What would you have done, huh? What would you have done if that had happened to one of your stock?"

Her eyes were wide. "Look. The key card was there, but there was no note. I swear it."

"And I swear I wrote it." He thought back, trying to remember leaving that night. He'd packed his things. Written the note. Grabbed some pizza and soda and gone out the door…

"It was windy," he said, quieter now. "The weather front was coming in. When I left, maybe it blew off the table. That's all I can think of, Kailey. I swear to you I wrote you a note. After last winter, did you really think I would just leave you in a motel room again?"

She looked down, and everything inside him suddenly felt heavy.

"You did. You really thought I had left you there. After all we shared this summer. After going with you to Lewiston, after making love to you…you thought I had just up and abandoned you without an explanation."

She lifted her chin. "I never saw any note. What was I supposed to think?"

So many answers rushed through his head. "I don't know, but the benefit of the doubt might have been nice. Or maybe answering my text. Or taking one of my many phone calls and giving me the chance to explain." He clenched his jaw. This wasn't going as planned.

"You really don't get it, do you?" she asked. "You hurt me. You humiliated me— again. This time in front of my employees. In front of a lot of people who knew you were there with me last week!"

"So, this is about your pride?" He cursed, frustrated and angry. "You know what, Kailey? I think I deserve a little portion of the hurt and anger that's being handed around. I was really starting to care for you. Do you think I would have gone to Lewiston with you otherwise? Really? But maybe this was more one-sided than I realized. Maybe you're so damned worried about appearances and being right that you can't see something when it's right in front of your face. I ran, yes. I ran to take care of my responsibilities. I left you to be with a horse that was ripped to shreds by a mountain lion and, by some miracle, survived. I wrote a note explaining my quick exit. I followed up with a text as soon as Rattler was treated, and I'd managed to get a few hours sleep after driving all night and then being with him all day. And what do I get for my trouble? Being told what a rotten human being I am and how your stupid pride took a beating. Just who is the coward, anyway?"

Her lips fell open and he half regretted being so harsh and the other half of him was relieved he'd gotten all that off his chest.

"You're putting this on *me*?"

He swallowed. The lump in his throat was growing, but he was tired of being the bad guy simply because of a bad judgment call six months ago. "I heard a saying a long time ago. I never knew what it meant until now."

"Oh, and what's that?"

He met her gaze evenly. "The real courage isn't in loving someone. It's allowing them to love you back. I know I made mistakes, Kailey, but I put myself out there. It's not me running away right now. It's you. You're the one who's scared. You're the one running in the other direction, and I'm the convenient scapegoat."

"You left me," she whispered hoarsely.

"You left me there like I meant less to you than a stupid horse."

He made a disgusted noise and took a step back. "Kailey, would you listen to yourself? You, who should understand most since you were asked to make that choice not that long ago. You told me Colt didn't understand why you couldn't leave the ranch. That it was an impossible choice to make. And now you're accusing me of caring more for Rattler than I do for you?"

She lifted her chin in response. He stepped forward now, cupped her saucy little chin in his hands. "Do you think that if you were hurt somewhere that I wouldn't move heaven and earth to find you?"

"I don't know that for sure."

He dropped her chin. "All this time I thought we could just take it slow and see what happened. I thought we could figure it out. That you'd forgiven me for my stupid mistake. That you could trust me again. But you don't. It's not just about trust, either. If you have that many doubts, you really don't know what kind of man I am at all."

No one had ever had any expectations where he was concerned. Or perhaps he hadn't expected enough of himself, either.

Of course, by holding everyone at arm's length, it kept him from being hurt.

There just came a time in a man's life, he realized, where he had to make a stand. And that time was now. It was time he decided what he wanted, time he stopped settling, time he started having his own expectations. For himself and for the people he cared about.

Kailey was still standing on the porch, barring the door, her arms crossed against her chest. Stubborn, stubborn woman. His anger was fading and in its place was disappointment. In their relationship. In her. That hurt most of all.

"At some point, Kailey, you're going to have to stop putting up walls and blaming everyone else. Ask yourself what you're really afraid of. Take it from someone who knows. Because I was like you. Never let anyone too close. Never show my hand. Until you. I fell in love with you. Are you brave enough to do something about it?"

Her face paled and her eyes glistened, but she didn't say anything. Disheartened, Rylan picked up his toolbox, turned around and went back to his truck. He shut the door and looked up, and she had gone back inside.

He backed out of the driveway and started toward home. Only one other time in his life did he remember feeling this heartbroken. And that was when they'd driven away from Crooked Valley, leaving their old life behind.

Well, maybe Kailey had broken his heart, but he could definitely do something about the second.

It was time he came home. Really came home, the way he'd been afraid to all these years.

Chapter 14

Kailey hung up the phone, her hand shaking and her heart heavy.

After Rylan had gone, she'd called the motel in Lewiston. It had been less than forty-eight hours since she'd checked out, and she knew housekeeping would have gone through the room. But if there was a chance the note still existed, she wanted to find out.

The room had been cleaned, the clerk had said, but they'd send someone to check to see if a slip of paper had been missed behind the desk or something, and they'd call her back. And they did, only twenty minutes later, with Rylan's note in hand. They read it to her over the phone and she'd closed her eyes, feeling sick about how she'd treated him.

She stared at the phone, wondering if she should call him and apologize, but she didn't. She sat on the sofa, her legs crossed and her elbows on her knees, thinking. This wasn't about missing a note he'd written. It was about faith and trust and fear, and she couldn't fix those with a simple phone call. Because that was about her, not Rylan.

And that was work she had to do on her own.

She threw herself into working at the ranch, and went along to two more rodeos during the month just to get away and clear her head.

But no matter how much she tried to sort out her feelings, she was reminded that Rylan, for all his declarations, hadn't even hinted at anything permanent. He had no plans to stay on at Crooked Valley, so where would that leave them even if they could work things out?

Setting herself up for more hurt, that's where. It would just be better if she kept her distance and worked at getting over him.

The days were getting shorter and the nights cooler, and she was spending a quiet Friday evening at home rather than heading out to the Silver Dollar. The bar didn't hold much allure these days, and her busy schedule made her appreciate a night to stay home in comfy leggings and a soft sweatshirt. But she was lonely, too. She was just contemplating putting in a DVD when there was a knock on the door.

Her heart leaped. Maybe Rylan had been as miserable as she'd been and wanted to talk. She'd avoided Crooked Valley altogether since their breakup and hadn't seen him. She ripped the ponytail holder from her hair and gave her head a brisk shake, squared her shoulders and went to answer the door.

It was Lacey and Carrie. Carrie was holding Evan in her arms, and had a diaper bag over her shoulder, while Lacey carried a bottle of wine, a box of chocolates and a bag of potato chips.

She held up her loot. "I have all the bases covered. You asking us in or what?"

Kailey stepped aside. "What is this? A pity party?" It was shameful how happy she was to see her friends. She really had isolated herself the past few weeks, hadn't she?

"An intervention. And since Carrie's nursing, she gets to play sober driver."

"Indeed," Carrie said, sliding the diaper bag off her shoulder. "My treat of the evening is some sort of fizzy lemonade that Lacey bought."

They went straight through to the living room, and Kailey stopped in the kitchen to retrieve two wineglasses, a corkscrew and a pretty glass for Carrie's beverage. In those few moments, Lacey had put all the food on the coffee table and Carrie was sitting in a cozy chair, Evan on her lap, his little fingers clutching a toy that looked like red, blue and yellow keys.

Lacey waggled her fingers for the corkscrew and Kailey handed it over. "Okay," she said. "What sort of intervention are we talking about?"

"A romantic one," Carrie said, her knee bouncing just a bit to keep Evan occupied. "Something happened between you and Rylan the weekend Rattler was attacked, and it occurred to us that both of you are miserable."

Kailey snorted. "I wouldn't say miserable." The wine opened with a pop and Lacey went straight to work, pouring two glasses. She handed one to Kailey.

"Miserable," Lacey confirmed. "Nothing else would explain you totally avoiding Crooked Valley for two solid weeks and never calling your best friends."

"It's been busy…"

"Sure," Carrie and Lacey replied in unison.

"It has. I've been to two rodeos, too. Out of town."

"Interesting. Since you rarely travel with the stock."

It was true. There was no sense in trying to fool either Carrie or Lacey. "Fine. I've been avoiding your place. It would just be awkward."

She took a sip of wine. Then another. Lacey poured the lemonade for Carrie and handed her the glass, then opened the box of chocolates and tore open the bag of chips. "Pick your poison," she stated.

Kailey reached for a dark chocolate truffle first. It went very nicely with the rich merlot and she leaned against the back of the sofa.

"Look, you guys, Rylan and I had a misunderstanding. Some of it was his fault. A lot of it was mine. But when we talked, I think we both realized there's a lot more wrong with us than we thought. Yeah, I've done some thinking, and it's just better this way. I mean, come Christmas Rylan will be gone to wherever, and it won't be an issue anymore."

Carrie and Lacey looked at each other, then back at Kailey. "Is that what you think? That Rylan's temporary and you'll just be able to forget him?" Lacey put her hand on Kailey's knee. "Honey, I was there the day he offered to pay for lunch at the diner. Things have never been easy for you. And one thing's for sure…you've never been indifferent to each other."

Kailey's heart hurt just talking about it. "Like I said. It doesn't matter. He'll be gone soon enough, right?"

Carrie's gaze was sympathetic. "Um, not exactly. He's staying on at Crooked Valley."

The second truffle seemed to catch in her throat and she took a quick gulp of wine to wash it down. "What do you mean?" she asked, her voice shaking a little. "Staying on how?"

"As in taking on his third," Lacey replied. "He told us nearly two weeks ago. He's going to take over managing the rough stock side of the ranch. I'm staying on as administrator, and Quinn and Duke are going to run the cattle operations."

"I'm going to pitch in whenever and however," Carrie added. "With Evan being so small, I'm really focusing on being mom right now. Plus—" she smiled a little bit "— we're thinking we'd like to have more than one."

Kailey blinked quickly and reached for another chocolate. Her friends were so happy. Why could she not find that? Or was what Rylan said true? Was she the one standing in her own way?

Rylan. Staying on at Crooked Valley. Which meant she'd never be able to truly forget him because they'd be neighbors. Neighbors in the same line of work. The idea of seeing him to talk business darned near gutted her. How could she face him, knowing how she felt about him?

"But..." She looked up at both women. "He always said he wasn't one for settling down in one place. That he doesn't want to be committed to anything or anyone."

I fell in love with you, he'd said. Had he

really meant it? Then there was the whole thing with Rattler. It wasn't just that it was his horse. He'd used words like responsibility and courage and home. Did that sound like a guy on the verge of running?

"He didn't," Lacey confirmed quietly. "Until now. He told us how difficult it was for him as a kid, being uprooted from here after our dad died. How he never fit in, never belonged anywhere. But he feels like he does now. Like he's part of something important, like he's where he's meant to be."

Bully for him and all his belonging and completeness.

"But he isn't happy, Kailey. Because there's something missing. He fell in love with you. And you're clearly miserable without him, so what gives?"

Kailey stared at them both for several seconds, then held out her glass. "Could I have some more wine, please?"

Lacey dutifully topped her up, added a splash to her own glass and put the bottle down again.

Kailey took a long drink. Gathered up her courage. Looked her friends in the eyes and admitted, "I'm a coward."

Carrie snorted while Lacey smiled affectionately. "Don't be silly. You're one of the bravest people I know."

"But I'm not. And Ry's the first person to ever call me on it. Do you want to know what really happened with Colt last fall?"

She paused, and saw that Carrie and Lacey hung on her every word. "Well, he proposed. And then he presented this whole future where I'd move to be closer to his work, and I couldn't believe he was asking me to leave Brandt. His assertion was that a wife should follow her husband, and he withdrew his proposal when I said I couldn't just up and leave the ranch. But know what? I've discovered two things. Colt wasn't the right person, because when the right person comes along you should be able to say you'll follow them anywhere, right? And the other thing I learned about myself is that I've been hiding behind Brandt Ranch so I don't have to put myself out there. Ry and I really aren't that different, you know. We just hid behind different things."

She gave a sheepish smile to her friends. It was time she faced the truth: the ranch made for a fine excuse when she wanted to distance herself from the possibility of getting hurt. Or more than that…looking weak.

Weakness, she discovered, or at least the appearance of weakness, was what she was truly afraid of.

Evan started to fuss and Carrie put down her glass and cuddled him close, trying to soothe his whimpers. "But why?" she asked softly. "Why would you feel you had to hide behind the ranch? You're smart and beautiful. Fun."

It meant a lot to hear her best friend say those things. "Carrie, you know what it's like. I've had to fight for credibility in the industry, especially taking on the leadership role that I have. I'll be the first to admit that I sometimes fight against being, well, feminine."

Lacey sighed. "Men. Just because you have breasts doesn't make you any less qualified."

Kailey laughed, feeling better at the unequivocal support. "Hey, you know that and I know that, but not everyone feels that way, and it's not just men either. But I love what I do, so I deal with it."

"Right." Carrie nodded. "Which is why you and I used to blow off steam at the Dollar now and again." Her cheeks colored a little. "Which I haven't really done since I got pregnant. Shoot, Kailey. I kind of abandoned you, didn't I?"

Kailey shook her head. "Your priorities shifted, that's all. I guess the other thing is, when I did cut loose—like you and I used to do, Carrie—I became Fun Kailey. I've gained a reputation of not being marriage material. I'm the best friend or the fling but not more than that. And over time, I suppose that I started to protect myself by not putting my feelings out there. Colt wasn't the first person to hurt my feelings. And Rylan certainly wasn't either."

But it had been different with Rylan, she realized. Her feelings for him must have been bigger and more intense than she thought, because she'd cried more tears over him than she ever had over Colt or any man, for that matter. Tears formed in the corners of her eyes. "Crap," she murmured. "I didn't want to do this. Get all emotional and stuff."

"Maybe that's exactly what you need," Lacey said, reaching over and taking her hand. "I get it, Kailey. My ex-husband left me pretty gun-shy about ever being in a relationship again. You build walls around yourself and tell yourself no one will ever get close enough to hurt you like that again."

Kailey gave a quick nod, fighting tears.

"It took Quinn really pushing me to make me start fighting for the life I wanted," Lacey continued. "So the big question is, what do you want?"

That, of everything, was the easiest thing to answer. "I want it all," she whispered, sniffling. "I love the ranch. I've worked so hard with my dad to turn it into what it is today. I don't want to leave it. And I want a man who loves me, and a family of my own. Maybe I just…want too much."

Lacey and Carrie both smiled. "Honey, you're not asking for too much," Carrie assured her. She'd discreetly settled Evan at her breast and smiled with beatific contentment. "Ranching isn't like a regular nine-to-five gig. Working the land means having a relationship with it, a connection that goes beyond a job. Brandt Ranch is part of who you are, plain and simple."

Kailey thought about that. "Maybe it's too much of me, though. Gosh, I don't know. I've been a real mess lately."

Lacey was the one who took everything down to the lowest common denominator. "Do you love him?"

She didn't have to ask if she meant Rylan.

Of course she did. The tears she'd succeeded in blinking away came back with a vengeance. "Maybe. Probably. And how dumb is that? I let myself fall for him when I knew he was leaving."

"But he's not leaving. And we hoped he wouldn't. We hoped that this would happen. That he'd come back here and see what a great place it is, that there's a home for him here. And he has." Lacey's gaze probed hers. "I truly think that he's needed to find his way back here all along. Are you going to punish him for that, K?"

"I'm scared he'll leave again."

Lacey nodded. "I know. And I can't convince you he's changed, and he can't convince you either, unless you allow yourself to believe it. To trust him."

Evan had fallen asleep and Carrie tucked him close in a soft blanket. "Sweetie, just think about it. You're miserable over here, and he's miserable over at Crooked Valley, and it's plain to all of us that you guys should be together. It might have started with a spark in February, but this summer it changed into something more. It wasn't just Rylan who changed. It was you. You changed each other, Kailey. And the beautiful thing is you never meant to. You were just yourselves."

Kailey was full-out crying now, tears slipping down her cheeks. "I was so terrible to him," she whispered. "I accused him of stuff that was just dumb, all because I was scared. How do you get the courage to really love someone?"

And then Ry's words came back to her. *Real courage isn't in loving someone. It's allowing them to love you back.*

The problem wasn't how she felt about him. She'd known for some time that she was in love with him. It was the act of letting him love her, giving him access to all her deepest secrets and desires. Letting herself be totally vulnerable and open.

Could she do it? Really? Could she not? How would she live next to him for the rest of her life knowing she'd blown her chance at happiness simply because she'd wanted guarantees that didn't exist?

"I've been an idiot," she whispered, looking up at her friends. "A real idiot."

"You can always stop doing that and make things right." Carrie's lips curved in a goofy smile. "We'll even help you."

"You will?"

"Of course." Lacey nodded. "Let's get down to business, then, shall we?" She held out her glass for a top up.

Kailey grabbed the bottle, topped off both their glasses and reached for a handful of chips.

Suddenly, the night didn't seem quite so hopeless.

Rylan sat on Duke's front porch, nursing a beer and wondering why things seemed so damned quiet.

It couldn't be because of Kailey. She belonged at Brandt, and even though she visited Crooked Valley frequently, it wasn't as though she was part of the daily routine. Maybe it was because it was fall, and things were slightly slower than they were in the middle of summer. Either way, Rylan knew two things. Staying at Crooked Valley was a good decision. One he felt happy about. As soon as he'd said the words to Duke and Lacey, he'd felt a sense of rightness wash over him. The second thing he knew was that he missed her. And that he was both angry and hurt over how things had gone down.

Duke and Quinn came out of the house,

each with a bottle of beer in their hands, and sat down in the other chairs on the porch, stretching out their jean-clad legs. "Nice night," Quinn remarked, and Duke agreed, and the three of them looked out over the ranch. Their domain. All three had a stake in it now.

"Where did your women go?" Rylan asked. "Figured at least one of them would be around, pesterin'." He tried a smile. It fell flat.

"They went out for a while. Left us on our own." Duke was close enough to nudge Rylan's elbow. "Peace and quiet."

Quinn shrugged. "I don't know. Seems too quiet around here without them around."

Rylan's mood darkened. They didn't know how lucky they were. The women they loved didn't hold one mistake against them for the rest of their damned lives.

"So," Quinn said, a little too conversationally to be coincidental. "This thing with Kailey."

"Is over." It stung even to say it.

"What'd you do?" Duke asked.

"Why did I have to do something?" Rylan retorted, swirling the beer around in his bottle.

"Because it's always our fault," Duke said reasonably. "Carrie rolls her eyes and tells me that men aren't as highly evolved as women."

Even Rylan had to give a bit of a chuckle at that. "Seems to me women appreciate a little caveman now and again," he replied, letting out a deep breath. He didn't need to take out his bad mood on his brothers. He already considered Quinn a brother, rather than a mere in-law.

Quinn took a drink, swallowed and rolled his head to look at Rylan. "You kind of blew it on Valentine's Day, bucko. You did a good job of fixing it until you ran out on her."

Rylan scowled. "I swear to God, I wrote a note, put it with the key card. It must have fallen behind the desk or something. And I texted and tried to call as soon as I knew Rattler was okay. I didn't just up and leave."

"To her you did."

"Dammit, I know that. But I explained…"

"Hey, we know you did. We're with you. But Kailey…she has a hard time trusting, period." Quinn frowned. "She's always felt she had to work twice as hard since her mom and dad had a daughter and not a son. She has high standards, Rylan. And people end up disappointing her, like that jackass Black."

"I'm not like that. I'd never ask her to walk away from Brandt. It's part of her. I know that much." He made a disgusted sound in his throat. Colt Black wasn't worth considering.

"I'm not saying she's right, Ry." Quinn let out a big breath. "But what I am saying is…don't give up. Not if you really love her. I know she's one of my best friends and I'm biased, but I think she's worth it."

"How many times do I beat my head against the wall, then?" Ry asked. "Because that's what I'm doing, and it doesn't feel very damn good."

Duke looked over at him and held his gaze. "As many as it takes," he answered simply.

They each took a long drink and stared off across the fields.

Chapter 15

"Hey, Rylan, someone from Brandt just phoned. One of their hands spotted a couple of our calves on the property line."

Rylan looked up from the paperwork he was doing and pinned a direct gaze on Lacey. "You're telling me this why? Quinn and Duke usually take care of this stuff. Calves aren't even supposed to be near that place. You sure they're ours?"

"Quite sure. Quinn's got his hands full, and Duke and Carrie have taken Evan in for his latest checkup. That leaves you."

"Can't one of the hands go?" Just what he wanted, treading the border line between their property and Kailey's. After his chat with Duke and Quinn the other night, he still didn't know what to do about her. His brothers had both said he needed to keep trying and show her how he felt, but after a while a man got tired of always feeling wrong and having a door slammed in his face.

Lacey put her hands on her hips. "For God's sake, it's a few little calves. Saddle up a horse and get the hell out of the barn. You could use some space and air. You're starting to be a real downer."

His irritation peaked and snapped. "Fine," he bit back. "Since everyone seems to have an opinion on what I should do with every moment of my day, I'll get on a horse and bring back your stupid calves."

"Thank you." She sounded incredibly pleased, which only infuriated him more. "You know where the creek takes that right angle bend? It was really close to there."

Great. Just what he needed. In case he hadn't been thinking about Kailey enough, he now had to go to the swimming hole where they'd shared some of their most memorable moments. Today was off to a great start.

He put the paperwork aside and brought

in Chief to be saddled, and then headed out
to the property edge in search of the lost
calves. How they'd been separated from the
herd, he had no idea. At least the September
weather was mild. The cottonwoods were
shedding their leaves so that the trees and
drying grasses were varied shades of brown
and gold, gilding everything with the warm
colors. Rylan exhaled, grudgingly admitted
that Lacey was right. He'd needed to get out
of the barn.

He scanned the rolling hills for any sign of
the calves, but so far he saw nothing. As he
rode along the edge of the creek, he listened
to the trickle of the water, the level lower
now than it had been earlier in the summer,
and thought of the times he'd come here with
Kailey. That first night he'd come upon her
swimming in her underwear and how he'd
joined her, making her blush. Other times
they'd met in the mellow evening heat,
cooled their hot skin in the cold water, making love in the pool and on a blanket on the
bank. He'd taken it, and her, for granted, and
now she was gone.

The creek slowed, widened and curved
around a huge old cottonwood, glowing with
golden leaves. And there, just around the

bend, stood Kailey, in a pair of jeans and a gray hooded jacket, holding the reins of her favorite mare—an aging Appaloosa named Sprinkles.

He reined in, stared at her from beneath his hat. "What are you doing here?" he called out. "You looking for those calves, too?"

But even as he asked, he knew it had all been a lie. Lacey had set this up. He loved his family. Staying on at Crooked Valley wasn't going to be a mistake. But if they thought meddling in his personal life was okay...

"There are no calves," she called back. "Your herd is miles from here." A soft smile lit her face. "Actually, I can't believe you fell for that line. It was Lacey's idea. I bet her it wouldn't work."

"I was distracted," he replied, trying to understand. So, Kailey and Lacey had been in on this together? But Kailey hadn't talked to him in days. Not since he'd walked away from her place after she'd returned from Lewiston.

"Apparently. I'm glad, though. I wanted to talk to you."

"You could have picked up the phone," he

said. A little part of him wanted to believe this was a good sign. But another remembered the harsh words she'd hurled at him, and he hesitated, staying firmly seated in the saddle.

The slight smile that had curved her mouth slid away. "Ry, I chose this place for a reason. It's middle ground, where your place and mine meet. Neutral territory."

Middle ground. Terms of peace but nothing more, right? Not the place where they'd begun the crazy slide into love, which was what he'd thought, for the briefest second, had been what she was going to say. His throat felt tight. He didn't dare get his hopes up one more time. She didn't trust him, and she'd made that perfectly clear the last time he saw her.

"Just say what you need to say," he advised.

Kailey stared up at the man on the horse. He seemed like such a stranger. The usual flirty half smile was gone from his face and his eyes were shadowed by the brim of his hat. Her heart beat a frantic tattoo as she wondered if this had been a big mistake. If she was too late.

But she'd been in the wrong. And it was up to her to apologize and make things right, if it was possible.

Her voice shook as she spoke, taking one step closer to Chief.

"I owe you a huge apology," she said, then cleared her throat. "For what happened after Lewiston. For jumping to conclusions. Though," she added, biting down on her lip for a moment, "the conclusions weren't that much of a stretch considering…"

That wasn't what she'd planned to say, and she stammered a bit and backtracked. "B-but I didn't believe you when you told me about the note. And I didn't forgive you and I should have. I'm sorry, Rylan. I really screwed things up."

His expression remained harsh, but she saw his Adam's apple bob and hoped he was feeling *something* right now. That he hadn't totally closed his heart to her.

"Say something," she whispered.

"You wanted to apologize?" he asked, his voice expressionless. "Make peace between the Hatfields and McCoys?"

She laughed. "We're hardly that, Rylan. I never hated you. There's no feud…"

"You sure don't love me," he replied

sharply. Too sharply. She stared at him, her lips open. She'd really, really hurt him. Strangely enough, the knowledge gave her hope. Indifference was her real enemy. If he cared enough to be hurt, maybe there was still a chance for them.

"That's where you're wrong," she replied. "Please, Rylan. Won't you get down from there and talk to me?"

He hesitated for a moment, but then swung his leg over the saddle and hopped down. He took off Chief's bridle, too, setting him free. Chief wouldn't go far, and he'd enjoy grazing for a while until Rylan called him to go home.

"You know I'm staying on at Crooked Valley, don't you?"

She nodded. "The girls told me. What made you change your mind?"

The leather and hardware of the bridle dangled from his hand. "I fought it for too long. Leaving it the first time gave me such bad memories I didn't want to come back again. Then once I was back—really back— I realized I was so determined to leave that I was cutting off my nose to spite my face. This place has always been my idea of home. I can still rodeo—I love it, too—but working with the stock, helping it grow...that's where I want to be."

He met her gaze and his eyes hardened. "I suppose that makes me more attractive now. That I'm not such a drifter."

She absorbed the hit. So defensive, so... hurt. She hadn't realized how sensitive he was, but perhaps she should have. All the things he'd told her had added up to a boy and man who didn't give too much of himself to anything so he didn't get hurt. But he'd given a lot of himself to her, and she'd thrown it back in his face.

And so she said the words she knew he needed to hear. And she meant them.

"Rylan Duggan, I fell in love with you when I was convinced that you were leaving again. When you disappeared for days on end, competing, and when you came back and had to face losing your championship hopes. I loved you every moment of this summer. Otherwise I never could have asked you to go along with me to Idaho. Don't you get that? I'm sorry I overreacted. I'm sorry I got scared and stubborn. And am I glad you're staying in Gibson? Well, maybe I am. Of course, that all depends."

"Depends on what?"

She stepped forward again until they were only a few feet apart. "It depends on what happens here. Right now, today. Because if you staying here means we're not together and I have to see you every day and see what I messed up because I was a coward, that's going to be really hard to live with."

His blue eyes flickered with some emotion she couldn't quite decipher, but it definitely wasn't indifference.

Encouraged, she took the final steps and fastened her fingers around the denim of his jacket. "Rylan, I ruined everything. I know that. And yeah, I'm scared. I'm really scared. I'm throwing away my security blanket here and giving you the power to hurt me. This is me. Just me. I have no idea what I'm doing and no idea what comes next, and that terrifies me, but I know one thing for sure. I love you. And you can do with that what you will. You can love me back, which, by the way, is what I hope you'll do. Or you can break my heart. Either way, it's yours."

And offering it to him was something she'd never, ever done before. She thought it would be crippling and terrifying, but in this moment, it felt utterly right to surrender it to something bigger than herself.

He dropped the bridle on the ground, then took off his hat and dropped it on top of the tack. "K," he said softly, and something in her chest seemed to take wing. She loved how he shortened her name to a single letter, how his eyes raked over her with a hunger that went beyond the physical. This was the Ry she remembered. Larger than life. Dangerous and wonderful.

"I'm sorry," she said again, and to her chagrin she started to cry. "I'm so sorry, Rylan. I turned you away instead of letting you in. I was such a fool."

He reached out and pulled her into his arms. "No more of a fool than I was," he replied roughly, his lips close to her ear as he held her close.

She clung to him for several seconds, absorbing his strength and heat and the sheer delight of his body close to hers once more. "Oh, I missed this," she murmured, tightening her arms around him.

"Me, too," he replied. He leaned back a little and brushed a thumb down her cheek. "But, Kailey, you were so sure you couldn't trust me. So angry. What changed?"

She looked up at him, knowing the time to lay herself bare had come and that she finally had to trust someone with everything. "I can't say it's any one defining moment," she said, staying in the circle of his arms. "Rather it's a lifetime of making the ranch my life. I'm a woman in a man's world. And the ranch is successful, so on some level that's threatening. At least that's what Colt said."

"Threatening?" Rylan laughed. "Honey, if we're talking about how capable and bossy you are, let me tell you, it's sexy as hell."

Her body warmed all over from the praise. "Not everyone is as liberated as you, Duggan. I fight for credibility in this industry, but now and again I have to blow off steam. I have no one to blame but myself. I'm the fun girl, you see. Not the keeper girl. Because the ranch always comes first."

Rylan frowned. "Do you realize how often you label yourself? Why do you do that? Why do you have to be anything other than just Kailey?"

No one in her life had ever asked her that before. "Ry, my parents are wonderful, but there has always been an unspoken ideal that I'm representing the ranch and have to act accordingly. Over time I suppose I've been afraid to show anyone the real me. Even my friends."

"And who is the real you, Kailey?"

She sank her hands into his hair and gazed into his eyes. "The real me is a rancher, a woman, someone who wants a lover and a family and a place to call home. And that woman would have scared you to death six months ago."

He closed his eyes briefly. "You did. Scare me to death, that is. That's why I left that morning, you know. I could see all of it in your eyes and it terrified me. God, we're peas in a pod, aren't we? So determined to never let anyone close, so we never get hurt."

"Except we couldn't stay away from each other."

"No. We couldn't. And then, of course, what I wanted changed. I had to stop running at some point. Crooked Valley was as good a place as any."

"And I had to open my heart to someone. I know you were telling the truth about the note. I admire what you did, too. It was responsible, honorable. Hell, Ry, it's what I would have done if Rattler had been my horse. I'm sorry I didn't believe you. I was just…"

"Scared," he finished. "And so was I."

"I have a hard time trusting, Rylan. But I can't keep holding on to that one mistake. Everything you've done since coming back to Crooked Valley has proved I can believe in you. And the rest I'll take on faith. I believe in you, Ry."

Finally, finally he said the words she'd been dying to hear.

"I love you, Kailey. I thought I could go through life not having to risk my heart to anyone, but then there you were. Stay or go, that won't change. I love you. And you've said you love me. All that remains is deciding what we're going to do about it."

He loved her. Her heart sent up a wild hosanna and a smile blossomed on her lips. "We can talk about the future later," she replied. Right now they had more important matters to take care of. "Can you please kiss me first, Rylan? I've been dying for you to kiss me again."

He cupped his hand around the back of her neck and pulled her close, kissing her with a singular intent that sent her heart racing.

"I love you," he murmured, sliding his lips

over the crest of her cheek. "And I missed you. So much."

"Me, too. Nothing was right..."

"I had everything I was supposed to want and it was gray and meaningless..."

"I thought I'd sent you away for good. Ruined everything..."

"Not a chance." His lips captured hers again and before long jackets dropped to the ground and their hands were skimming over warm skin, dying to be close once more.

"It's cool out here," he proclaimed. "I don't want this to be rushed and prickly on the grass and whatever else. I want to love you properly, Kailey. I want to make up for lost time and make things right."

She ran her hands over his shoulder blades, loving the feel of the warm skin beneath his shirt. "You're going to make me wait?"

He captured her arms and his fingers circled her wrists. "Only for a little while. I need you to listen to me first, okay? Because I don't want to be the one to screw things up this time."

"Okay," she agreed.

He twined his fingers with hers. "Kailey Brandt," he said, his gaze clinging to hers,

"I was not looking for love. You weren't on my radar at all. And I was dreading seeing you again when I came back in May. I knew I'd been a total ass in February. I definitely didn't deserve for you to give me another chance. But you did."

He squeezed her fingers. "I told myself it was fun and light and easy, but I knew exactly what I was in for when you asked me to go to Idaho with you. That night before I left…something changed. There was a moment when I looked in your eyes and I could see my future laid out in front of me. I wasn't scared anymore. I wanted to go home, look after Rattler, and figure out how everything fit together. I wasn't prepared for you, sweetheart. Not prepared, not looking. And suddenly there you were."

Her eyes stung, touched by the sincerity in his voice and gaze.

"I know you're scared. I'm scared, too. Scared to love you. Scared I might disappoint you. Scared I'm not the man you deserve."

His lip wobbled, and she sniffed, trying to hold herself together but not sure how long she could.

"I've never trusted anyone, not since I was

five years old. But I trust you, Kailey. I love you. And somehow we'll make it all come together. You somehow became my everything. My reason for breathing, my light in the darkness."

How long had she been waiting for someone to say those words to her, to mean them, to love her so much he couldn't go on without her? She was deliriously happy and humbled by it, and she held tight to his hands as she responded. "You're my everything, too, Rylan. Nothing seems to work when you're not in my life."

His eyes were troubled, though, as he gazed down at her. "I can't just up and leave Crooked Valley, though. I have to stay to take on my third, which will ensure Lacey and Duke's futures. I need to do that for them. I need to know I...I did something important. I can't be the add-on anymore."

"You're no afterthought. Especially not to me, Ry. You know that, right?"

His eyes softened. "I'm working on believing you. And I love hearing you say it."

She touched his cheek. "We'll figure it out. The most important thing is we're together."

She remembered saying to Lacey and

Carrie that when a person loved another, they should be willing to follow them anywhere. Right now, in this moment, she knew that she would make that sacrifice to be with Rylan. He was *the* one. She also knew that he would never ask her to make that sacrifice, because he understood her better than anyone she'd ever known.

Which was exactly how she'd always believed it should be.

"Rylan?"

"Yes, honey?"

She tilted up her chin and smiled. "Is this a proposal?"

The sideways grin she loved crept up his cheek. "Well, shoot. It would be if you let me get to it."

While the horses grazed nearby and the creek burbled over the rocks, Rylan got down on one knee and Kailey put her hand over her mouth, thrilled and surprised and overwhelmed that her greatest hopes had come true.

"Kailey, will you marry me? I don't know what the future holds, but I promise I want to be the one standing beside you as we find out."

She nodded, tears clogging her throat and

preventing her from answering. But she figured he got the answer anyway as he stood up and she launched herself at him, wrapping her arms around his neck.

Eight months later

The spring roundup was in full swing. Today the event was at Crooked Valley. Local ranchers, including the Brandts, all pitched in to help Duke and the rest of the crew brand, vaccinate and neuter cattle. It was busy, dusty, dirty, tiring work, and at the end of the day Lacey and Carrie put on a huge spread of food including grilled ribs, cornbread, baked beans and a smorgasbord of other delights that were guaranteed to please workers and neighbors alike.

Amber, now finishing kindergarten and ready to move into first grade, was in charge of plates, napkins and cutlery and made sure everything was replenished for the workers. Carrie spooned up the beans, Evan's head peeking out over the top of a baby backpack. Kailey grinned at the sight of the red curls and touched her tummy, wondering when the right time would be to tell Rylan the good news. She'd just taken the test two days ago, and figured they'd get today over with before he got to play protective daddy.

Lacey was working the grill, basting the ribs with her homemade sauce, and Kailey watched as Quinn stepped up behind her and wrapped an arm around her waist. He said something and Lacey laughed, then they shared a quick kiss before he moved on again. Recently they'd begun the screening process for adopting, hoping for a brother or sister for Amber.

A year and a half ago, Joe had been ill and the future of the ranch had been uncertain. Now it was full of life again, and children, and hope.

"Hello, gorgeous." A pair of strong hands came to rest on her shoulders. "Tired?" He gave her shoulders a little rub and she let out a satisfied breath.

"A little. Good day, though. Days like today remind me what ranching is supposed to be like. And community."

"Me, too. I'd forgotten for a long time, I think."

She turned her head and looked up at him, his strong jawline and twinkling eyes. Her husband for the past seven months. Their wedding had been low-key and lovely. Neither had wanted a long engagement or a big production. A month after the proposal, they'd tied the knot in the country church with only their families in attendance, and then had gone back to the Brandt house for a homemade prime rib dinner. Their honeymoon had been spent in Glacier National Park, a romantic three nights in the mountains sleeping in the cozy quarters of Rylan's camper. Since then they'd moved into Quinn's house—the bungalow was a convenient halfway mark between the Brandt and Duggan properties. Instead of selling off the bucking stock side business, they'd come to an agreement with Brandt and operated as a subcontractor, so both ranches reaped the benefits without being in competition with each other.

"Do you need to stay late tonight?" she asked. As good as the day had been, she was tired, and could use some quiet time. Like a warm bath and a cuddle on the couch with her favorite cowboy.

"I should be good to go by eight or so."

"Sounds fine."

Duke strolled by, dirty from head to toe, and gave Ry a slap on the back. "Hey, you newlyweds. It's about time you got on with the baby-making business, don't you think?"

Kailey saw him wink at Carrie, and with a laugh she patted her tummy and then raised her eyebrows at Rylan and Kailey.

"Wait," Kailey said. "Are you saying that you and Carrie…"

Duke's grin was huge. "We said we wanted to have our kids close together. So they'd grow up together."

He looked at Rylan as he said it, and the brothers shared a look that a year ago never would have happened. So many fences had been rebuilt within the family, all due to Joe's crazy will.

"Congrats," Rylan replied, shaking his brother's hand.

"Well, you're a healthy lookin' guy. No reason why this should be taking so long."

Kailey's heart pounded in anticipation. "Um, who said it was taking too long?"

Duke stared, but she only had eyes for her husband. All it took was a quick nod on her part and he let out a whoop that could be heard all over the farm yard. "When?" he asked her, and she laughed.

"I found out a couple of days ago."

He picked her up and swung her around.

When he set her down again, she saw Duke grinning at Carrie and patting his belly to share the news and Quinn and Lacey grinning at them like idiots while Amber piped up, "Why is everyone smiling?"

It was Rylan, the man who just a year ago had driven into Crooked Valley with no intention of staying, or falling in love, or making plans for the future, who answered her.

"You're gonna have another cousin, sweetheart."

Amber was off, telling the good news to anyone who would listen, and Rylan turned back to Kailey and looked into her eyes. "Are we ready for this?"

She smiled at him and shrugged. "Rylan, when have we ever been ready for anything? We just take it as it comes. And it all works out right."

He tucked a piece of hair behind her ear. "Jeez, for someone who had trust issues, you've really learned to take a lot on faith."

"All because of you," she murmured, gazing up into his eyes. "All because of you."

* * * * *

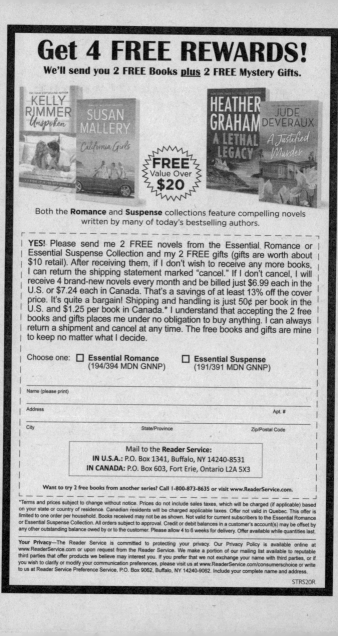

ReaderService.com has a new look!

We have refreshed our website and
we want to share our new look with you.
Head over to ReaderService.com
and check it out!

On ReaderService.com, you can:

- Try 2 free books from any series
- Access risk-free special offers
- View your account history & manage payments
- Browse the latest Bonus Bucks catalog

Don't miss out!

If you want to stay up-to-date on the latest at the Reader Service and enjoy more Harlequin content, make sure you've signed up for our monthly News & Notes email newsletter. Sign up online at ReaderService.com.